THE XIII WINTER OLYMPIC GAMES

LAKE PLACID 1980

From the approach highway near Lake Placid, the clear outlines of the ski trails and slopes on Whiteface Mountain can be seen (preceding page). The trails near the top of Whiteface will be used for downhill and slalom competitions during the 1980 Winter Olympic Games.

TABLE OF CONTENTS

Editorial Director, JAMES KUSE
Managing Editor, RALPH LUEDTKE
Production Editor/Manager, RICHARD LAWSON
Photograpic Editor, GERALD KOSER
Copy Editor, SHARON STYLE

Designed by DAVID SCHANSBERG
and MARTY ZENS
Written by GALE BRENNAN
and DAVID SCHANSBERG

ISBN 0-89542-013-9 595

11315 WATERTOWN PLANK ROAD, MILWAUKEE, WISCONSIN 53226

PRINTED AND BOUND IN THE UNITED STATES OF AMERICA
PUBLISHED SIMULTANEOUSLY IN CANADA

The quiet, little village of Lake Placid is comfortably nestled in the Adirondack Mountains of New York on the shores of Mirror Lake (partially visible above) and Lake Placid.

A COMPLICATED CHALLENGE

From February 12 to 24, 1980, the tiny community of Lake Placid, New York will be the sports center of the world.

Is it possible that a small town nestled in the Adirondacks at the foot of Whiteface Mountain can host the Olympics? Can its dedicated citizens, sparse in number, handle the myriad of details necessary to conduct a world spectacle? Can the people and the area cope with athletes, coaches, officials, foreign dignitaries, state and United States government officials, along with international press, radio and television crews who will cover the site like locusts? Does Lake Placid have the facilities, the weather, enough electrical outlets, plumbing, and housing facilities? No matter the travail, hardships, risks, and multitude of challenges, the community, which attained national prominence when it hosted the 1932 Winter Olympics, will once again emerge bright and shining and intact, a winner. Somehow, you just knew this would happen all along! Olympic organizers have coined the slogan: "The Olympics in Perspective." They intend to provide spectators the lowest priority and return to a more "homey" Olympic atmosphere, much the same as it was in 1932.

However, the number of events has more than doubled; there are four times as many participants, and the number of media personnel who will cover events for press and television have multiplied more than a hundredfold, as there may be fifty to one hundred technicians assigned to provide sound and camera coverage for each event.

There obviously will be a severe shortage of living quarters not only in Lake Placid, but for one hundred miles in any direction. Plans call for printing 51,000 tickets for each day's events, 28,000 of which will be offered for sale to the public. The rest will go to corporate sponsors and local residents. Of the 28,000, approximately half will be apportioned to tour operators, who will sell them in packages including lodging and transportation. During the Olympics, parking on Lake Placid streets is totally banned; outlying parking lots with shuttle buses are handling transport. The aim of the various committees is to provide a low-key atmosphere for Olympic competition. A further objective is to make this project a financial success. Based on "track records" of other cities in the world which have hosted the Olympics, if the latter can be achieved, everyone involved in the Lake Placid area deserves gold medals. Even with the sharpest pencils and most professional budget-conscious supervision, when *any* event calls for a $150 million "up-front" outlay, the prospect for breaking even is, at best, chancy.

While admittedly a big tab, the $150 million projected for the 1980 Olympic Winter Games is far less than the $400 million spent for the Winter Olympics at Grenoble, France, and the $700 million for the Games in Sapporo, Japan. Federal, state, and private support, including television rights, admissions, and commercial advertising rights, together with other assorted income revenue sources, are expected to meet budget needs.

Lake Placid already has many of the necessary competition facilities. The area includes the state-operated Whiteface Mountain ski area, ten miles east, and the Mount Van Hoevenberg Recreational Area,

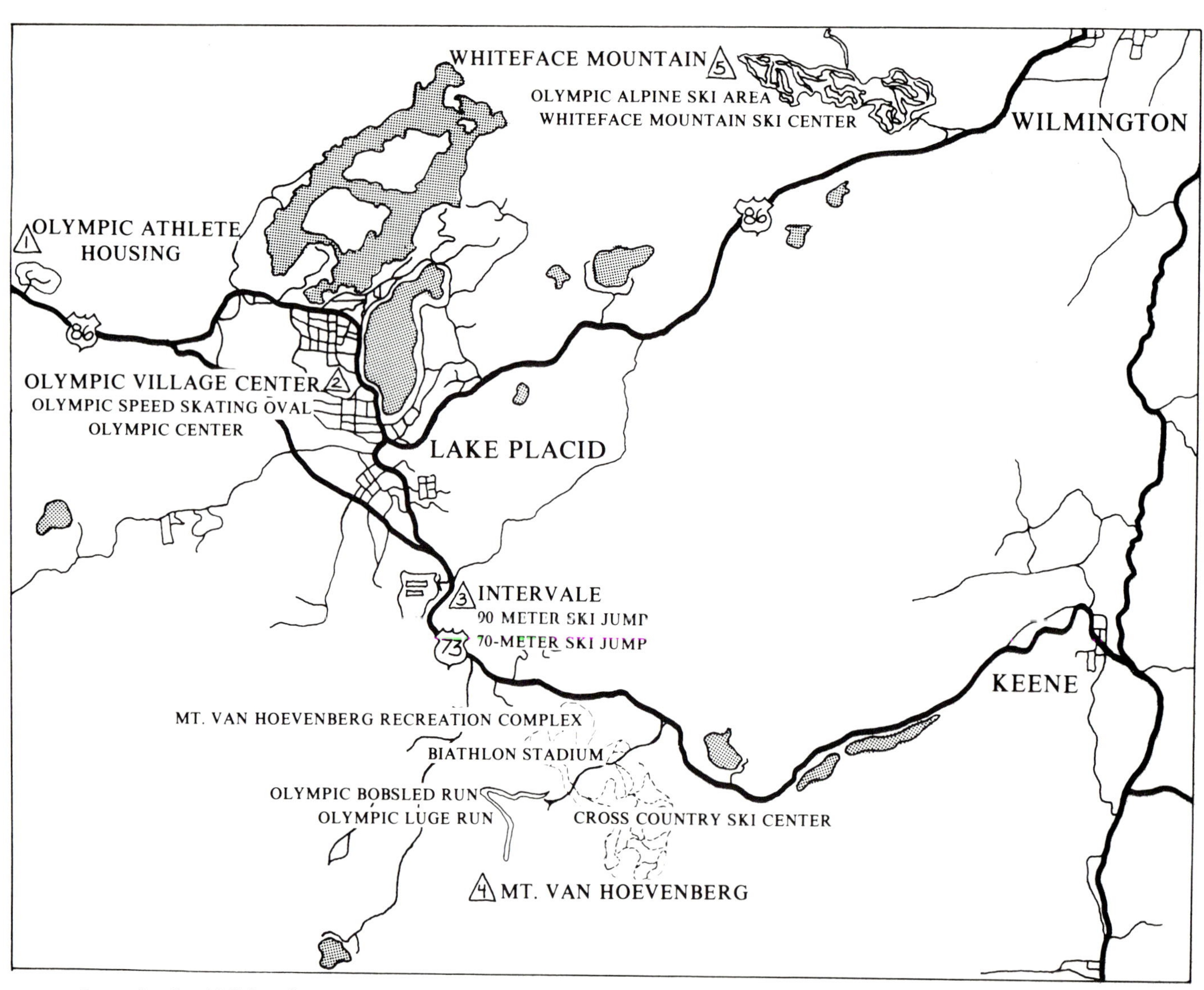

maps drawn by David Schansberg

six and one-half miles south. Alpine ski events will take place on Whiteface, whereas cross-country, biathlon, bobsled, and luge events will be run on the established Mount Van Hoevenberg courses. Speed skating will be conducted on Lake Placid's outdoor Olympic skating oval; hockey and figure skating will take place in the 1932 Olympic arena, which has been completely renovated. Ski jumping will commence from new 70 and 90-meter ski jumps at Intervale, a mile south of the city. Government contractors have constructed Olympic Village, seven miles west of Lake Placid. It is slated to become a minimum security prison following conclusion of the Games.

An unbelievably tough, complicated task for what is basically a small American village? Most assuredly, but a number of residual benefits accrue to the community hosting Olympic Games. Once a bobsled run is constructed, it stays. So do ski jumps, arenas, housing facilities, and any other structures built to accommodate and facilitate Olympic competition. Since Lake Placid is currently a widely known and well-patronized tourist and winter resort area, it will reap benefits far into the future. The immediate "cash flow" won't be unwelcome either!

The 1980 Winter Olympics in prospective—where heroes will be born, champions will be vanquished, records will be set, victors will be crowned, and losers will weep.

1980 WINTER OLYMPIC SCHEDULE

TUESDAY, FEB. 12

Ice Hockey—Olympic Center (two rinks) 13:00-13:30
16:30-17:00
20:00-20:30

WEDNESDAY, FEB. 13

Opening Ceremony Lake Placid High School Sports Stadium 14:30
Luge: men's and women's 1st run—Mt. Van Hoevenberg 19:00

THURSDAY, FEB. 14

Speed Skating: women's 1500-meter—Olympic Oval 10:30
Alpine Skiing: men's downhill—Whiteface Mountain 11:30
Cross-Country Skiing: men's 30-kilometer—Mt. Van Hoevenberg 09:00
Luge—Men's and women's 2nd run—Mt. Van Hoevenberg 19:00
Ice Hockey—Olympic Center (two rinks) 13:00-13:30
16:30-17:00
20:00-20:30
Awards Ceremonies—Mirror Lake 19:30

FRIDAY, FEB. 15

Figure Skating: ice dance, 2 compulsory dances—Olympic Center 14:00
pairs short program—Olympic Center 21:00
Speed Skating: men's and women's 500-meter—Olympic Oval 10:30
Cross-Country Skiing: women's 5-kilometer—Mt. Van Hoevenberg 09:00
Bobsled: two-man 1st and 2nd run—Mt. Van Hoevenberg 09:30
Luge: men's and women's 3rd run—Mt. Van Hoevenberg 14:00
Awards Ceremonies—Mirror Lake 19:30

SATURDAY, FEB. 16

Speed Skating: men's 5,000-meter—Olympic Oval 10:30
Biathlon: individual 20-kilometer—Mt. Van Hoevenberg 09:00
Bobsled: two-man 3rd and 4th run—Mt. Van Hoevenberg 09:30
Luge: men's and women's 4th run—Mt. Van Hoevenberg 14:00
Ice Hockey—Olympic Center (two rinks) 13:00-13:30
16:30-17:00
20:00-20:30
Awards Ceremonies—Mirror Lake 19:30

Schedule continued on page 77

FOR THE GLORY OF SPORT

Traditions are built slowly and carefully and generally are not based on written instructions. Traditions are never manufactured, they are passed on and handed down from generation to generation.

The Opening and Closing Ceremonies of every Olympic Games are solidly rooted in tradition. No matter where the Games are held, or what individuals comprise the various committees, ceremonies which signify the opening and closing of competition seldom stray from a form that has been nurtured, developed, and abided by through the years.

Olympic officials welcome athletes, dignitaries, and spectators to the 1976 Winter Olympics and proclaim the Games open as the Olympic Flag is slowly raised (above). After the welcoming ceremony, the torch arrives via runner, and the Olympic fires are ignited to burn high above Innsbruck, Austria, for the duration of the Games (left).

When the Sovereign or Chief of State arrives at the Olympic site, he is received at the entrance by the President of the International Olympic Committee and the President of the Organizing Committee. Members of these respective committees are presented to him, after which he is conducted to his box. There he is greeted with the national anthem of his country.

The now-famous "parade of the participants" follows. Each contingent, dressed in official uniform and preceded by a shield bearing the name of the country, begins the march. The flag of each nation is carried in front of its team; contingents parade in alphabetical order, except that Greece always leads and the host nation's teams bring up the rear. Competitors salute the Sovereign or Chief of State by turning their heads toward his box. All flags and shields are of equal size. After the march around the stadium, each contingent lines up on the center of the

Izumi Tsujimura skates into the Sapporo, Japan Olympic Stadium with the flaming torch on the last leg of the relay from Greece. She delivered the torch to Hideki Takada, who took it to the top of the stadium to ignite the giant brazier, officially opening the 1972 Winter Games. The host country is responsible for assigning runners (or skaters) to participate in the relay.

field and maintains its position in a column behind its shield and flag, facing the Tribune of Honor.

Olympic officials proceed to a rostrum on the field in front of the Tribune of Honor, where the President of the International Olympic Committee is introduced. The President of the IOC mounts the rostrum, delivers a brief welcoming speech, and requests the Sovereign or Chief of State to "proclaim open the Games of the Olympiad." The Sovereign or Chief of State then says: "I declare open the Olympic Games of . . . celebrating the . . . Olympiad of the modern era." Immediately, a fanfare of trumpets is sounded. As the strains of the Olympic "Anthem" fill the air, the Olympic Flag is slowly raised. A symbolic release of pigeons then occurs, followed by a three-gun salute. At this moment, the Olympic Flame arrives, brought from Olympia via a relay of runners, the last of whom circles the track and lights the sacred Olympic Fire, which is not extinguished until the close of the Games.

An athlete representing the nation where the Games are taking place advances to the rostrum, accompanied by the flag bearer of his country. He mounts the rostrum, and holding a corner of the flag in his left hand, raises his right hand and takes the following oath on behalf of all competitors: "In the name of all competitors, I promise that we will take part in these Olympic Games, respecting and abiding by the rules which govern them, in the true spirit of sportsmanship, for the glory of sport and the honor of our teams." The national anthem of the organizing country is then played or sung, while participants leave the arena.

The competition begins!

A special corps of selected runners will carry the Olympic flame from Langley AFB, Virginia to Lake Placid, New York, where it will remain lit until the 1980 Olympic Games are concluded. The flame is ignited by the rays of the sun at Olympia in Greece. It is then flown to the nation hosting the Olympic Games, then hand carried to the site of the Games along a route selected by Olympic officials.

Runners have the symbolic responsibility of insuring that the flame is brought safely and with great dignity through cities and towns. The route for the 1980 Olympic Games has been chosen to give recognition to the heritage of the United States, according

to George Christian Ortloff, chief of ceremonies for the XIII Olympics. The landing site in Virginia is the home of the first English speaking settlement in the New World, and the historic victory at Yorktown, which ended the War of Independence. The route passes the birthplaces of George and Martha Washington and gravesites of eight presidents. The cities of Washington, D.C., Philadelphia, and New York through which runners will pass, have all been capitals of the nation. Most of the running will be done on roads which date back to the founding of the United States. Runners will pass through the hearts of cities, towns, and farmlands. According to Ortloff, every foot of the way provides a gorgeous setting and is a pathway to Lake Placid that will show off the best of both rural and urban America.

Requirements for the "carrier-runners" are not unduly stringent. Participants are not limited to competitive runners; each must be a citizen of the United States and at least sixteen years of age in 1980. Each must be able to traverse two kilometers (1.25 miles) while carrying a 5 to 6 pound torch aloft in no more than 12 minutes under winter conditions. Tests and rehearsals have been held during 1979 to familiarize runners with their duties, routes, and responsibilities.

To carry the Olympic torch part of the way to the Olympic site is an honor, part of an ancient tradition, and something to be cherished for a lifetime.

6

ICE HOCKEY

GLIDING ON GOLDEN BLADES

Some years back a moderately successful movie was produced entitled "The Russians Are Coming . . . The Russians Are Coming." With regard to the 1980 Olympic Ice Hockey competition, in fact, all world hockey, let it be known that "the Russians are here," and their domination in the sport is likely to continue indefinitely.

Hockey's historical roots began with a game played by Englishmen in Kingston Harbour, Ontario, in 1860. This was the first time a puck was used instead of a ball, which differentiated the game from field hockey. In 1879, a pair of Montreal students devised the game's rules, adding ideas to a combination of field hockey and rugby rules. This led to the formation, in 1880, of the first recognized team, McGill University Hockey Club. By the time the first game was played in the United States in 1893, more than one hundred clubs were thriving in Montreal alone. Lord Stanley of Preston, Governor-General of Canada, donated the Stanley Cup, destined to become one of the most recognizable and sought-after trophies in the sports world.

The first Olympic title and the first amateur World championship was won by Canada at Antwerp, Belgium, in 1920. Canada proceeded to win every Olympic title until 1936, when Great Britain defeated the Canadians at Garmisch, Germany. The Russians first began challenging the supremacy of Canadian teams when the USSR won the Olympic tournament at Cortina in 1956.

In the Soviet Union, hockey is an outgrowth of the political system. All the best young hockey players in the country live in Moscow and participate in an official state hockey program, which includes an intensive training regimen. According to expert observers, the Soviets' training program places far more emphasis on skating and finesse, rather than shooting or body checking. Russian hockey players are tremendous skaters, with remarkably similar styles. Their acceleration comes from short, choppy strides, almost like sprints, whereas Canadian and United States' skaters develop long, loping strides. In the USSR hockey programs are closely coached and monitored, frequently by players who competed in previous Olympics. This degree of emphasis on recruiting and coaching is in stark contrast to United States collegiate play which, while hotly contested, hardly qualifies its contestants to a place on a professional hockey team.

Last July, a tournament was conducted at the United States Air Force Academy. It served as a screening process to evaluate the top eighty amateur American hockey players prior to the selection of the 1980 Olympic team. This tourney uncovered a good deal of collegiate talent, but the team is given little or no hope of upsetting the Russians. Notre Dame coach Lefty Smith, who handled one of the teams competing, stated: "It [the tournament] has been a great benefit to the Olympic Games." Based on their performances, probable members of the next United States hockey squad will be: Mark Johnson, Wisconsin (son of the 1976 Olympic team coach); Joe Mullen, Boston College; Kevin Zappia, Clarkson; Bill Baker and Steve Christoff, Minnesota; Denver's Craig Roehl, and goalie Mike Dibble.

Even the best of American amateurs can't hold a hockey stick to the cream of the carefully groomed, highly trained Soviets. However, despite all the odds and pre-

The goalie and a defenseman from the Russian ice hockey team watch helplessly as the puck sails into the net they are defending (preceding page). The score was one of the few the Russian team has allowed in the four consecutive years in which they have won the Olympic gold medal in hockey. They are heavy favorites to win their fifth straight gold medal at Lake Placid.

The Russian ice hockey team poses with their gold medals after clinching their third consecutive Olympic championship in 1972 at Sapporo, Japan. They won again in 1976 and are expected to defeat all challengers at Lake Placid.

Olympic predictions, strange things can happen in competition. The most startling upset during the 1960 Games was the victory scored by the United States hockey team, which won its first and only Olympic medal. With a team considered a rank outsider in the competition, the United States' skaters went undefeated, toppling the Czechs, the Swedes, the Germans, the Canadians, the Russians, and the Czechs once again, to win the gold.

While the solid rubber hockey puck can take funny bounces, the Russians appear a shoo-in at Lake Placid, with all other teams vying for second or third.

Nonetheless, American amateur hockey fans, along with those of other nations, look back to the 1960 Olympics, when a similar set of circumstances prevailed. Is it possible that a newly assembled group of outstanding college hockey players can rise to the heights as a team? It happened twenty years ago. Flashing blades on the ice at Lake Placid will spell out the answer—in gold.

ICE HOCKEY

1920	Canada, U.S., Czechoslovakia
1924	Canada, U.S., Great Britain
1928	Canada, Sweden, Switzerland
1932	Canada, U.S., Germany
1936	Great Britain, Canada, U.S.
1948	Canada, Czechoslovakia, Switzerland
1952	Canada, U.S., Sweden
1956	USSR, U.S., Canada
1960	U.S., Canada, USSR
1964	USSR, Sweden, Czechoslovakia
1968	USSR, Czechoslovakia, Canada
1972	USSR, U.S., Czechoslovakia,
1976	USSR, Czechoslovakia, W. Germany

LUGE

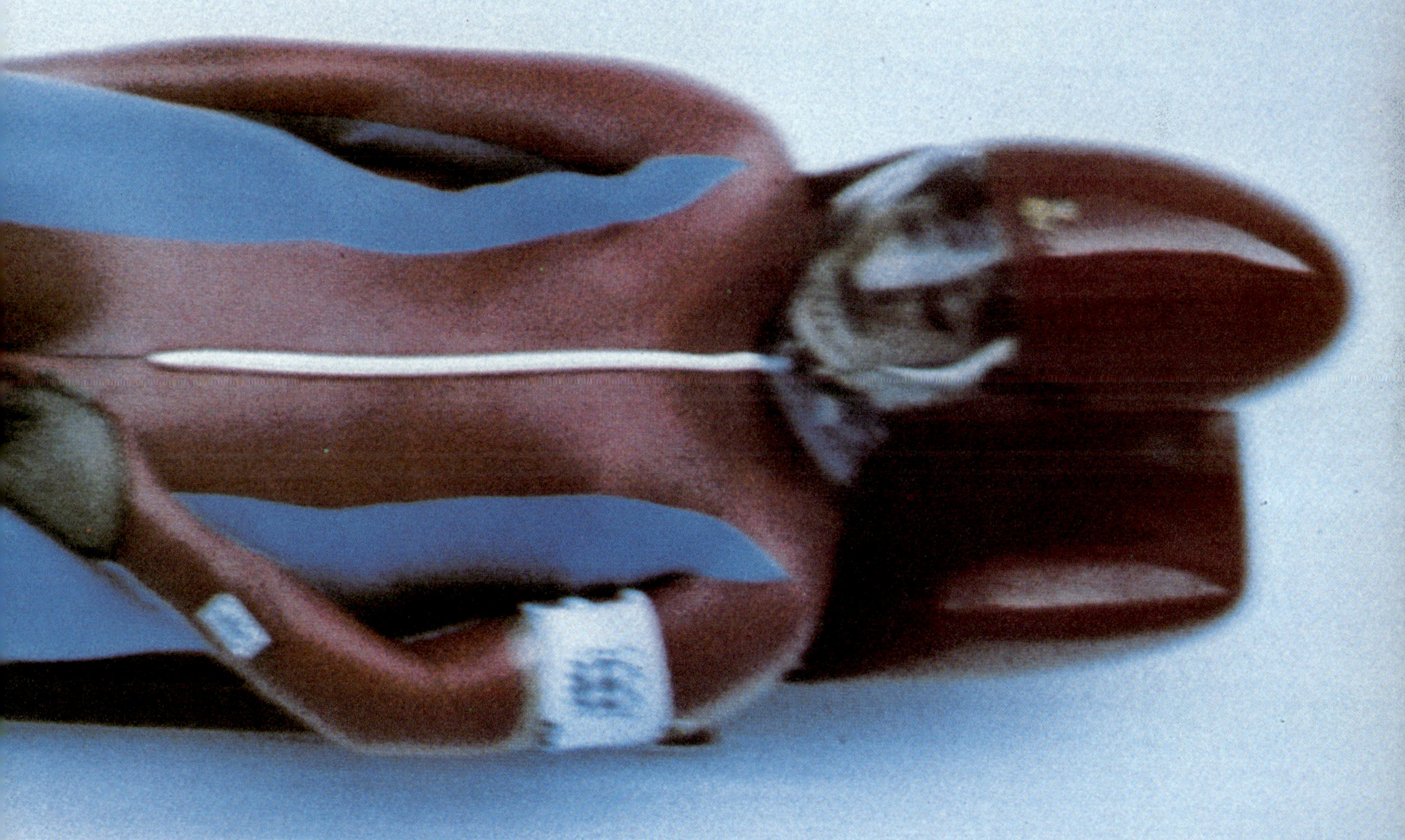

The United States has constructed a new luge run, 1,000 meters long, curving and coiling through the trees on Mount Van Hoevenberg near Lake Placid, New York. This $4.5 million structure of concrete, steel, and wood was built for the 1980 Winter Olympic Games. Jan Steler, a French-Polish architect, designed the sculptured, refrigerated run regarded by experts as perhaps the best luge run in the world. Certainly it is the best in the Western Hemisphere, since it's the only one—an obvious reason why luging is dominated by European teams.

The history of luge racing dates back to the middle 1880s, when mountain roads in the European Alps were used for sled racing. These "fun runs" eventually evolved into serious competition, when various groups challenged each other.

The first European luge championships were held in 1914 at Reichenfeld, Austria. The luge sleds were stiff, and the tobogganer steered by touching the ground with his gloved hands, studded with small iron points. In Norway and Switzerland, a twelve-foot-long flagstaff was used as a rudder; this proved hard to handle. In the 1930s, a big advance in the sport occurred with the invention of the flexible sled. Luging possibilities became as great as those with a bobsled, as everything was now done by the body, requiring nothing mechanical. The luge competitor makes three movements to steer the sled: pulling up the inward runner, pushing the front end of the outward runner to the inside, and placing weight on the outward runner, making it go faster than the inward runner. It is up to the tobogganer to select the right combination for each straightaway and curve. Luge runs, where speeds have been clocked at up to 80 miles-per-hour, are similar to bobsled runs, except they are steeper and the corners are narrower. With no mechanical means of steering or braking, the luge toboggan must not exceed twenty kilogrammes in weight nor one and a half meters in length.

A member of the East German women's luge team rockets to a gold medal through a curving course of ice, at speeds approaching 90 miles-per-hour (preceding page). The elongated helmet, unique to the East German team, helps make the single unit of rider and sled more aerodynamically efficient. Apparently it works; the East Germans have swept all three luging gold medals for two consecutive Olympics.

Addition of the luge sledding event to Olympic competition was decided by the International Olympic Committee meeting in Athens in 1954. It became part of the Olympic competition in 1964 at Igls, Austria. Controversy plagued the event when several crashes, one fatal, occurred during training sessions preceding the opening of the 1964 Winter Games. With course and equipment evaluations, and the subsequent changes made, the luge event is now considered no more dangerous than bobsledding.

The East Germans have long dominated this exacting sport. In the four Olympic Games since the single and double luges were first included among official events, East German riders have won twenty of the thirty-six Olympic medals awarded.

The Russians, however, have made a breakthrough and are expected to be a major factor in the 1980 Games. The USSR launched an expensive national program in the early 1970s, building six luge courses in arctic regions of Russian land, then spent additional funds recruiting and developing "super-lugers," who are determined to bring home gold medals from the 1980 Games.

Detlef Gunther of East Germany is the reigning Olympic gold medalist and is favored to repeat; USSR's Vladimir Shitov figures to provide Gunther with his strongest competition. Other East Germans, including the women's team are favored to sweep luge events at Lake Placid, with Americans far behind.

Now that an admittedly great Olympic luge run has been constructed in the United States, it is possible within the foreseeable future some stocking-capped American youngster will surely be destined to battle on even terms with the more experienced, well-traveled East Germans and Russians. After all, the name of the sport is "luge," not lose!

MEN'S SINGLES

1964	Thomas Kohler, Germany	3:26.77
1968	Manfred Schmid, Austria	2:52.48
1972	Wolfgang Scheidel, E. Germany	3:27.58
1976	Detlef Guenther, E. Germany	3:27.688

MEN'S DOUBLES

1964	Austria	1:41.62
1968	East Germany	1:35.85
1972	Italy, E. Germany (tie)	1:28.35
1976	E. Germany	1:25.604

WOMEN'S SINGLES

1964	Ortun Enderlein, Germany	3:24.67
1968	Erica Lechner, Italy	2:28.66
1972	Anna M. Muller, E. Germany	2:59.18
1976	Margit Schumann, E. Germany	2:50.621

Wolfgang Scheidel and Michael Kohler of East Germany appear out of control as they skid along the side bank during a two-man competition. Although the expressions on the two men's faces might indicate otherwise, the two are very much in control, as they use their bodies to maneuver the sled through the tricky turns of the run.

COUPE DU
FILA
7
VAL

ALPINE SKIING

GOOD CHANCE AT WHITEFACE

A pair of skis reputed to be 5,000 years old is on display in a Stockholm museum. Fashioned from animal bones, they were used primarily as a means of transportation in snow-covered countries. The enterprising inventor of skis hardly envisioned the purposes his creations would serve in 1980. The originators of Alpine ski racing, somewhat surprisingly, were British skiers, who under the guidance of Sir Arnold Lunn, established the world's first downhill race in 1911 at Montana, Switzerland.

At first competitors raced together, with the first one flashing past the finish line declared the winner. Due to the high speeds reached, along with the dangers from bumping and entanglement, this type of competition was abolished in favor of "racing against the clock," with the victor decided on total elapsed time.

Downhill courses are set with length, steepness, and degree of difficulty appropriate to the skills of competitors. The average championship course has a vertical descent of between 2,500 and 3,000 feet, with its length varying from 1½ to 3 miles. Today's skiers average more than 50 miles-per-hour; Jean-Claude Killy won the Olympic downhill in 1968 at Grenoble, France, averaging 53.93 miles-per-hour. However, skiers exceed 100 miles-per-hour on steep courses. In downhill skiing, the objective is to get from top to bottom in the quickest possible time, with the competitor free to select whatever route he considers most suitable to achieve that goal. Racers are permitted to practice on a downhill course and acquaint themselves with its characteristics before a race.

Slalom courses are much shorter than downhill and consist of a series of pairs of poles with flags, which are known as "gates." These are carefully positioned at different angles to test judgment, fluency of movement, power of control, skill in turning, and pace-checking, rather than sheer speed alone. Distance between the two flags of each gate is at least 10 feet; the flags rise 6 feet above the snow to be clearly visible. A skier who misses a gate is disqualified unless he climbs back and passes through it. Championship courses have from 50 to 75 gates and a vertical drop of between 650 and 975 feet; women's courses are shorter. A slalom event normally consists of two runs, either over the same course or different tracks, with the winner determined by the fastest aggregate time. Giant slalom courses blend characteristics of the downhill and slalom in one event; the trail is longer than the slalom, and the gates are set wider and farther apart. In contrast to downhill races, slalom competitors are not permitted to practice on the course previous to the official race. They

If recent World competition results are a reliable indication, and they usually are, Ingemar Stenmark of Sweden will probably win the Olympic slalom and giant slalom events with relative ease. Stenmark displays the smooth, aggressive style that has made him master of the slalom (preceding page). Stenmark was favored to win in 1976 at Innsbruck, but crashed early in the competition. Since that unfortunate performance, Stenmark has gracefully established himself as one of the all-time greatest Alpine racers. He won three straight World Cup Championships, the last by a record number of points. Winning two straight World Cup races, or several in the course of a season, is considered an outstanding achievement. In 1977, Stenmark competed in fifty-six World Cup races, and finished in the top three forty-two times. In twenty-six slaloms, he finished first fourteen times. Stenmark began the last World Cup season with seven straight slalom and giant slalom victories, a feat unmatched in ski racing history. In February 1979, he slammed through the gates with his customary power and elegance to win the slalom and giant slalom in the World Alpine Ski Championships. Stenmark has left the unmistakable impression that nobody does it better. The king of Alpine racing will be in the forefront of the skiing competition at Lake Placid.

Cindy Nelson of Lutsen, Minnesota carries the United States colors as she leads the American Olympic team into Berg Isel ski jump arena during the opening ceremonies of the 1976 Winter Games at Innsbruck, Austria. Nelson, the most experienced veteran on the Alpine team, will lead an improved American ski team into the 1980 Olympics at Lake Placid.

must attempt to memorize gate positions while ascending to the starting point. The slalom is essentially a test of technical skiing skill, while the downhill event places a higher demand on courage and fitness.

America has never had a gold medalist in a men's Olympic Alpine skiing event. The high hopes of breaking past tradition will rest primarily on the shoulders of identical twins Phil and Steve Mahre of White Pass, Washington. Their competition will be extremely tough, but the Mahre brothers have the best shot at winning America's first gold medal in men's Alpine skiing. The Austrians are likely to win the downhill and Ingemar Stenmark, the sensational Swede, will probably win both slalom events. Stenmark refuses to participate in the downhill. If he didn't, he would probably join Toni Sailer of Austria and Jean-Claude Killy as the only triple gold medal winners. Sailor swept all three events in 1956; Killy repeated the feat in 1968.

For the past several years Americans have become increasingly competitive with the Europeans, who have superior natural conditions on which to train, and widespread public support for their sport. Although the women's Alpine skiing events have also been dominated by Europeans, particularly those from Austria, Switzerland, and West Germany, the United States women's team has consistently out-skied their male counterparts in Olympic competition.

When women's skiing was added to the Alpine events in 1948, Gretchen Fraser, a daring perfectionist from Washington, captured America's first skiing gold medal.

Fraser had been selected to compete in the 1940 Games, but the events were cancelled. The 1944 Games did not take place. Almost thirty and after not winning a major race for six years, Fraser resumed competitive skiing as the next Olympiad approached. Unknown and a decided underdog when she arrived in Europe, she quickly startled the experts by winning the silver in the combined Alpine event. In the slalom, Gretchen skied magnificently, leaving the entire field far behind to snatch the gold medal.

Another outstanding Olympic performance was turned in by American Andrea Mead Lawrence. She became the first skier to win two Alpine events, by taking the gold in both the slalom and special slalom in 1952. Barbara Cochrane was the first American to win a gold medal since Lawrence turned the trick twenty years earlier. American women have done relatively well in Olympic skiing competition and with the fine team that will represent the United States in Lake Placid, even more gold may be in store.

Annemarie Moser-Proell of Austria glides through the gates with the technically flawless style that has made her the pre-Olympic favorite to win a gold medal at Lake Placid. Moser-Proell won five consecutive World Cup Downhill championships (1970 to 1975) before retiring from competitive skiing. After a two-year absence, she returned to compete at the World Alpine Ski Championships in Garmisch, West Germany, last winter. Moser-Proell regained her form to win the downhill and combined championships to capture her sixth overall World Cup Championship. There are many up and coming women racers, but Moser-Proell remains the perennial Alpine queen.

THE WORLD CUP TEST

Upon taking their first look at the Alpine courses at Whiteface Mountain near Lake Placid, several of the European coaches felt the layout was inferior to world-class competition standards. At best the slopes might make a good cross-country run, they captiously remarked. Many racers believed the machine-made, snow-covered, downhill course to be flat, boring, and less than technically sound. The slaloms were simply not tricky enough.

How deceiving first impressions can be. After one day of training on the two, "flat," downhill courses, at speeds in excess of 87 miles-per-hour, most of the coaches and skiers were persuaded to change their opinions.

The best European and American skiers had gathered on the slopes of Whiteface in February 1979 for two reasons: to compete in another race on the World Cup pre-Olympic circuit and to test the site of the 1980 Olympic Alpine skiing competition. Ingemar Stenmark, the incredible slalom specialist from Sweden, came as did premier downhill champion Franz Klammer and his unpredictable, and often unbeatable, Austrian teammates. America's highest Olympic hopes, Phil Mahre and Cindy Nelson, were also on hand. The incomparable Annemarie Moser-Proell left the restaurant she operates in Austria to compete for her sixth World Cup downhill championship in seven tries. Winner of the 1972 Olympic Gold medal and grandmother of competitive skiing, Marie Theres Nadig came to prime her not-so-brittle bones for her third Olympic Competition. Consistent success at the World championship level is a prerequisite for recognition as a possible Olympic medal winner. These racers are proven winners and the top contenders for Olympic gold.

The World Cup events at Lake Placid laid to rest any skepticism about inadequate courses, and proved that at the 1980 Olympics there would be no shortage of thrills, spills, and fierce competition.

In the women's downhill, Nelson, in her eighth year of World class racing for the United States team, consistently clocked impressive times during the week of practice before the competition. Her training times were faster than those of everyone, including Austria's perennial downhill queen, Moser-Proell. Moser-Proell was a formidable opponent with amazing credentials. She had won five of the six previous downhills (Nelson won the other), has won a record five World Cup championships, fifty-eight World Cup wins, and has received eight Olympic or World Championship medals. But Nelson was ready and appeared to be a sure bet on her native snow.

On the day of the competition, Nelson was not capable of repeating her outstanding practice performances. Moser-Proell raced a mediocre run down the sun-soaked, sloppy slopes that held up for the next eleven racers. Then came Nelson, slamming through the top part of the course at an interval time two-tenths of a second faster than Moser-Proell. Unfortunately at the bottom of the run, her skis began to bog down in the mushy snow, and she slowed down tremendously. In the last thirty-three seconds of the race, she lost more than a full second to Moser-Proell. She finished eighth, the best United States finish. In conditions where the application of ski wax outweighs the application of the skiers, Annemarie Moser-Proell had obviously outwaxed the field for another World Cup championship. She was followed by Marie Theres Nadig and Bernadette Zurbriggen. The Swiss teammates helped keep their team high in the team standings.

Austria's dominance of the downhill was carried to a further degree by the men. Franz Klammer, a surprise gold medalist at the Innsbruck Olympics in 1976, is experiencing an unexplainable series of poor performances

Marie-Theres Nadig of Switzerland is under full steam as she completes a practice run for a World Cup Downhill race. Nadig has been one of the world's greatest women skiers for several years. She won two gold medals at the 1972 Olympics in the slalom and giant slalom. Although that was eight years ago, Nadig is still considered a top contender for the gold at Lake Placid. In 1979 she finished second only to Annemarie Moser-Proell on the World Cup circuit.

that began almost two years ago. Klammer has slipped to the bottom of the Austrian downhill team. Joseph Walcher, who trained for the downhill by watching films of Klammer in his prime, has consistently done well in World competition. Last year Walcher edged out his teammate to capture the World Cup downhill. He had done his homework well. But at Lake Placid it was still another Austrian who would carry on the tradition of fine performances. Peter Wirnsberger glided fearlessly over the icy run to win the downhill, leaving with the second World Cup win of his career. Klammer continued his trend, finishing a disappointing nineteenth.

There was more at stake than a pre-Olympic medal in the men's giant slalom. The overall World Cup championship was still undecided, making the race at Lake Placid crucial. In 1978, Stenmark had the overall championship wrapped up by the end of January. Stenmark turned on his awesome power and usual technical finesse to repeat as champion in the slalom and giant slalom, winning the latter by an incredible two-second lead. But Stenmark was ineligible to win the overall championship because of a new set of rules instituted at the beginning of the 1979 season. In an effort to bring back the vaunted three-event performer a'la Jean-Claude Killy or Karl Schranz, the new rules were designed to reward the competitors who raced in all three events: downhill, slalom, and giant slalom. A competitor who enters only one or two events cannot possibly accumulate enough points over the course of a season to win the overall championship. Stenmark considers downhill an event unfit for civilized man and refuses to enter in it, despite being the undisputed king of competitive racing.

The two leading point winners were unheralded Peter Luscher of Switzerland and American Phil Mahre, second to Stenmark on the tour last year. But the spirited rivalry was to end at Whiteface. Mahre, realizing that a good race could catch Luscher in the point standings, began to run with his characteristic calculated recklessness. After passing the midpoint, Mahre caught a gate with his ski and crashed. America's primary gold medal hope had broken the tibia in his left leg. Luscher went on to finish third in the giant slalom and win his first World Cup championship. The excitement of the World Cup is a promising preview of the fierce competition which will pervade the Olympic scene at Whiteface. At the forefront of that excitement will be Ingemar Stenmark.

evian
1

Franz Klammer sails through another downhill run (left). Klammer won the gold medal in the downhill at Innsbruck, but in recent seasons he has only managed to turn in mediocre performances. However, Klammer's relentless style makes him a threat on any downhill. On a good day, Klammer could repeat his outstanding performance of four years ago. Should Klammer fail, his Austrian teammates are likely to bail him out. Jean-Claude Killy (above) was the last triple gold medal winner, having swept all three events in the 1968 Olympics at Grenoble. Toni Sailer recorded the only other three gold sweep in 1956.

MEN'S GIANT SLALOM

1952	Stein Eriksen, Norway	2:25.0
1956	Anton Sailer, Austria	3:00.1
1960	Roger Staub, Switzerland	1:48.3
1964	Francois Bonilieu, France	1:46.7
1968	Jean Claude Killy, France	3:29.28
1972	Gustavo Thoeni, Italy	3.09.62
1976	Heini Hemmi, Switzerland	3:26.97

MEN'S SLALOM

1948	Edi Reinalter, Switzerland	2:10.3
1952	Othmar Schneider, Austria	2:00.0
1956	Anton Sailer, Austria	194.7 pts.
1960	Ernst Hinterseer, Austria	2:08.9
1964	Josef Stiegler, Austria	2:11.13
1968	Jean Claude Killy, France	1:39.73
1972	Francesco Fernandez Ochoa, Spain	1:49.27
1976	Piero Gros, Italy	2:03.29

MEN'S DOWNHILL

1948	Henri Oreiller, France	2:55.0
1952	Zeno Colo, Italy	2:30.8
1956	Anton Sailer, Austria	2:52.2
1960	Jean Vuarnet, France	2:06.0
1964	Egon Zimmermann, Austria	2:18.16
1968	Jean Claude Killy, France	1:59.85
1972	Bernhard Russi, Switzerland	1:51.43
1976	Franz Klammer, Austria	1:45.73

Phil Mahre

Steve Mahre

DOUBLING THE CHANCES FOR A GOLD

In the first United States Olympics in twenty years, American fans may find themselves cheering wildly over not one, but two electrifying young racers. Phil Mahre and his identical twin brother Steve, twenty-one-years-old, of White Pass, Washington, are the best racing prospects this country has ever had. They are a fiercely independent, low-key pair with the identical highly polished ski technique that walks the fine line between a perfect run and a skidding crash.

Ever since they achieved national attention as a pair of daring, hard-skiing fifteen-year-olds in junior competition, their promise has been the hope of the United States team. Phil, the more dashing and reckless racer of the two, has been near the top of World Cup racing for a couple of seasons. Steve was reluctant to leave the comforts of home for the months of grueling tension and long hours of travel demanded of a serious World class competitor. But after edging into World class competition in 1977, Steve developed quickly and improved greatly.

The United States has experienced a less than glorious past in World Cup competition, the major preparatory races of the Olympic Games. Only Billy Kidd and Tyler Palmer have been able to win as many as two World

Whiteface Mountain is the site of the Winter Olympic Alpine skiing competitions. A strong field of competitors will battle for the gold on the slopes nearest the top of the mountain.

Cup races in their entire careers. Greg Jones and Bobby Cochrane each managed to win one. In the 1976-1977 season, only Phil's second, he won a World Cup slalom and a giant slalom. Last season he added two slaloms and a giant slalom to that record. In addition, Phil placed so consistently in last year's competition that he finished second in the overall standings behind Sweden's Ingmar Stenmark.

After Steve decided to enter the competition in 1977 he wasted little time in cutting loose. In a triumph unprecedented for brothers in ski race history, Steve finished third behind his brother, who took first, and Stenmark, who took second, in a World Cup slalom at Sun Valley. Last season Steve finished a very creditable eighth in the slalom at the Federation International Ski World Championships at Garmisch, West Germany, before flying through the gates at Stratton, Vermont, to beat both his brother and Stenmark, to win his first World Cup race.

The Mahre twins grew up twenty yards from the foot of the main chair lift of the White Pass ski area in Washington's beautiful Cascade Mountains. The resort was managed by their father, although he never pressured his sons to compete. At eight, both boys entered their first race. Phil finished first, Steve second—an early indication of what was in store for the two.

The twins insist they are hometown mountain boys at heart. "Wuss" and "Puss" as their high school pals nicknamed them long ago, would rather spend their time at a motorcross race or playing basketball with friends, than tolerating the rigorous demands and hassles of the World Cup circuit. Both were married last summer (not a double wedding) to their high school sweethearts, and now reside within six miles of one another in the quiet little community of Yakima in the apple orchards of Washington's Yakima Valley.

But the Mahres are committed to racing in the 1980 Olympics. They sound no great symphonies of patriotism in talking of the Games, only the desire to find enjoyment from the sport they love. That enjoyment may double the pleasure for the United States ski teams at Lake Placid. The United States men's Alpine team has never produced a gold medal winner in the fifty-six year history of the Olympics. But if the "Great White Pass Hope" can deliver on a promise, the United States stands twice as good a chance to win a gold medal in 1980.

Cindy Nelson

Christin Cooper

Susie Patterson

Viki Fleckenstein

Jamie Kurlander

Abbi Fisher

Becky Dorsey

The success of the United States Women's Alpine Ski Team in 1978 and 1979 World Cup competition has proven their ability to compete and win against the best racers in the world, many of whom will be participating in the 1980 Olympics. The women's team has been strengthened because much of the talent has arrived at the same time, creating competition within the team. All of the team members who won World Cup points last season will return this year to represent the United States at Lake Placid. The team is extremely talented and with a little luck, they could surprise everyone on the slopes of Whiteface Mountain. The 1980 United States Olympic Team is composed of:

CINDY NELSON—By way of her bronze medal in the 1976 Olympics at Innsbruck, Austria, Cindy became the greatest downhill racer America has ever known. Her second place finish in the 1978 World Cup downhill standings was the best ever by a United States racer. Cindy, twenty-two, from Lutsen, Minnesota, is the most experienced and consistent member on the team. She joined the team in 1971 and since that time has won five National Championships: the United States Downhill Championships in 1973 and 1978; the United States Slalom Championships in 1975 and 1976, and the United States Combined Championships in 1978. She was on the United States Olympic Team in 1972, 1976, and will again lead the United States into the 1980 Olympics.

BECKY DORSEY—Becky, twenty-two, from Menham, Massachusetts, was named to the team in 1973. Her expertise is in the giant slalom, where she won the National Championships in 1975, 1977, and 1978. She also won the 1978 United States National Slalom Championship. Becky is currently ranked seventh in the world for slalom and ninth for giant slalom. She is an aggressive skier with a great deal of determination.

SUSIE PATTERSON—Susie has been a ski team member for four years. She was a member of the 1976 United States Olympic Team, and was the 1974 United States National Slalom Champion and the 1976 United States National Downhill champion. Her brother Peter is on the men's Alpine team.

United States Women's Alpine Ski Team member, Susie Patterson.

ABBI FISHER—Abbi, twenty-one, from Conway, New Hampshire, was a member of the 1976 United States Olympic Team, and has been a member of the United States team since 1975. In the past two seasons Abbi has consistently finished in the top five in slalom and giant slalom World Cup events. She possesses enormous talent, but has been slowed in the past by injuries. With some luck she could win a medal.

VIKI FLECKENSTEIN—Although she has only been a team member for two years, Viki gets stronger and better with each race. In 1976, she was the Overall Winner of the Canadian-American Trophy Series and National Combined Champion. She is an excellent technical skier, and if she continues to improve as she has, she may be in contention for a medal.

JAMIE KURLANDER—Jamie, twenty-one from McAfee, New Jersey, has been with the team since 1977. She has done very well in World Cup downhill races but is versatile and competitive enough to participate in all three Alpine events.

CHRISTIN COOPER—Christin is the youngest member on the women's team. She was the 1977 United States National Slalom Champion and the 1976 Canadian-American Trophy Series Slalom Champion. Christin, nineteen, possesses a flawless technique that makes here a threat in either slalom event. Her big strength is in the turns.

WOMEN'S DOWNHILL

1948	Heidi Schlunegger, Switzerland	2:28.3
1952	Trude Jochum-Beiser, Austria	1:47.1
1956	Madeline Bethod, Switzerland	1:40.7
1960	Heidi Biebl, Germany	1:37.6
1964	Christi Haas, Austria	1:55.3
1968	Olga Pall, Austria	1:40.87
1972	Marie Theres Nadig, Switzerland	1:36.68
1976	Rosi Mittermaier, W. Germany	1:46.16

WOMEN'S GIANT SLALOM

1952	Andrea Mead Lawrence, U.S.	2:06.8
1956	Ossi Reichert, Germany	1:56.5
1960	Yvonne Ruegg, Switzerland	1:39.9
1964	Marielle Goitschel, France	1:52.2
1968	Nancy Greene, Canada	1:51.97
1972	Marie Theres Nadig, Switzerland	1:29.90
1976	Kathy Kreiner, Canada	1:29.13

WOMEN'S SLALOM

1948	Gretchen Fraser, U.S.	1:57.2
1952	Andrea Mead Lawrence, U.S.	2:10.6
1956	Renee Colliard, Switzerland	112.3 pts.

1960	Anne Heggtveigt, Canada	1:49.6
1964	Christine Goitschel, France	1:35.11
1968	Marielle Goitschel, France	1:25.86
1972	Barbara Cochran, U.S.	1:31.24
1976	Rosi Mittermaier, W. Germany	1:30.54

Rosi Mittermaier of West Germany turned in the finest women's skiing performance in Olympic history at Innsbruck in 1976. She shattered the Olympic record in the slalom to win her first gold medal. She failed to set a record in the downhill, but her flawless run was good enough for her second gold medal, making her the third woman to ever win two skiing gold medals in the same Olympic year. (Andrea Mead-Lawrence of the United States won double golds in 1952 and Marie-Theres Nadig accomplished the feat in 1972.) Mittermaier missed the unprecedented gold medal sweep when she lost to Kathy Kreiner of Canada in the giant slalom by a slim eighteen-one hundredths of a second. She is ineligible to compete with the West German team at Lake Placid, because she lost her amateur status when she signed a professional contract with an American ski manufacturer.

FIGURE SKATING

Olympic figure skating competition consists of two separate and distinct parts—compulsory and freestyle. The freestyle portion, featuring spectacular jumps, spins, and leaps, fascinates stadium crowds and millions of television viewers. By contrast, the "compulsory" portion (worth about forty percent of the final points scored) fascinates only the steely-eyed judges, many of whom get down on their hands and knees to study "tracings" left in the ice by the competitor. During the "compulsories," spectators stay away from the site rink in droves—and therefore witness only a little more than half of the way skaters are judged.

Compulsory skating requires solo competitors to trace with their skates up to six specific figures drawn from an internationally recognized schedule. Each compulsory figure is started from a stationary "rest" position and is composed of a prescribed pattern in the form of either a "two-lobe or three-lobe eight." The figures vary greatly in degree of difficulty, and are drawn to suit the standard of the event. Each compulsory figure is skated three times, each tracing an identation on the ice. Judges carefully examine the tracings made by the competitor's skates, and also judge the skater's control, posture, and balance maintained while making the tracings. The position of hands, fingers, even the non-skating foot are considered, along with the rate of a smooth, steady speed, and the change from one foot to another. "Bulging," or "flatting," or an improper change from one blade edge to the other costs tenths of a point.

"Free skating," as the name suggests, offers the competitor complete freedom of choice and movement, and an opportunity to insert original skills into his performance. As the climax of the competition, free skating permits a combination of precise edges and turns learned in figures to create intricate footwork embellished with jumps and spins. The performer is not restricted in what he may attempt, how he performs, or in what sequence he puts his "act" together. It is highly theatrical, allows the performer to display his "personality" along with his skating skill, and results in performances spectators enthusiastically appreciate.

Tai Babilonia and Randy Gardner polish and refine their pair's routine for the upcoming Olympics (preceding page). The pair won the bronze medal in the 1977-1978 World competition and are the reigning three-time National Pair's Champions. If Babilonia and Gardner continue to improve, they stand a chance to end the Russian's four Olympiad reign as pair's figure skating champions.

Several former figure skating champions, American Dick Button and Parisian Jacqueline du Bief among them, believe that "figures," which must be learned as the solid basis of technique, should have no bearing on the championship, and that "free skating" should become the sole criterion for judging. This is a highly contested issue.

Few people are aware that men's, women's, and pair's figure skating contests preceded other Olympic competition by sixteen years. Olympic medals in these three figure skating categories were awarded in 1908, pre-dating the opening of the first Olympic Winter Games in 1924. London was the site of the 1908 Olympic Games, during which Sweden's Ulrich Salchow won the men's figure skating event and Britain's Madge Syers captured the women's title. Heinrich Burger and Anna Hubler of Germany won the pair's event. The second Olympic competition in figure skating took place in Antwerp in 1920. It was the first international competition to attract American skaters, who were represented by Nathaniel Niles and Theresa Weld. Sweden's Gilles Grafstrom, originator of the flying sit spin, won the first of three consecutive gold medals in the men's event. The most successful pair in figure skating have been Oleg Protopopov and Ludmila Belousova, twice Olympic and four-time World champions.

While she never won an Oscar for her performances in a series of highly promoted Hollywood Ice Extravaganzas, Sonja Henie did much for the sport of figure skating. The

Sonja Henie's stylish imagination and innovative technique revolutionized the sport of figure skating and won for her a special place in the hearts of fans throughout the world. The tiny Norwegian (right) is the only woman to ever win three straight Olympic crowns (1928, 1932, and 1936). Her determination to excel became evident very early. Sonja mastered the dull "school figures," or compulsories, to win the Oslo women's championship at age nine and the Norwegian title a year later. At age ten, she also competed in her first Olympics at Chamonix, France, in 1924. Freestyle skating had been traditionally stiff and formal, so the judges found Sonja's added dimension of dance hard to accept. Although she received last place, the spectators were captivated and thrilled by this new, artistic form of skating. Figure skating was never to be the same. After winning her third gold medal, she toured the world and drew capacity crowds wherever she went. Sonja started and starred in her own ice show, becoming the first Olympic ice skating star to turn professional, and blazing the trail for all that have followed. She skated through ten films, making her one of the most popular Hollywood box office attractions in the early 1940s. Nobody has done more for the sport of figure skating than the incredible Sonja Henie.

diminutive Norway ice queen, Henie still rates as the most outstanding performer in women's Olympic history. Golden Sonja won three Olympic gold medals, in 1928, 1932, and 1936, and to this day is the only three-time gold medal winner in that competition. Perhaps Sonja Henie's major contribution to figure skating, in addition to her grace and skills, was to focus attention on this strenuous, demanding, and time-honored sport.

Linda Fratianne, at nineteen, is a two-time National figure skating champion and the 1977 World champion. Beginning her career, she placed seventh in the United States national figure skating championships at fourteen; and she has an excellent chance for a gold medal at Lake Placid. Linda is the fifth American since 1953 to win the World title. Tenley Albright reigned in 1953 and 1955; Carol Heiss won five in a row, from 1955 to 1960; Peggy Fleming collected three

John Curry's dramatic grace earned the gold medal in men's figure skating at Innsbruck (left). He will not compete at Lake Placid because he signed a professional figure skating contract. Fellow Britain Robin Cousins and American Charles Tickner are expected to be the strongest contenders in the 1980 event. Irina Rodnina and Alexander Zaitev of Russia (below) display the flowing, confident style that won the gold medal in the pairs competition at Innsbruck. Rodnina was also half of the combination that won in the 1972 Olympic gold medal, and she has won the World pairs competition for the last ten years, equaling Sonja Henie's 1927 to 1936 record in the women's event. Rodnina and Zaitzev will be out to capture the gold at Lake Placid.

straight titles, 1966 to 1968; and Dorothy Hamill added the World title to her Olympic laurels in 1976. Working hard and improving her skills through constant training, Linda Fratianne will be a tough, but graceful, contender for the gold in 1980.

Charles Tickner, representing the United States at the 1978 World figure skating championships in Ottawa, won the gold medal in the men's competition and is expected to vie for the Olympic gold in 1980. During his prize-winning performance, Tickner executed four triple jumps and two difficult double axels that brought his routine to a dazzling climax. Tickner has attracted world renown, however, much of it has been less than positive. At twenty-four, the "grand old man of the United States' skaters," Tickner has been close to the top for years but has also built a reputation for finding a way to lose. His upset win at the World figure skating championships in Ottawa might be just what the talented skater needs to stand center-stage on the Olympic pedestal. Until this cherished win, Tickner had a history of erratic performances. At the 1974 national championships, he fell twice and cracked a skate blade. In the 1976 nationals, he crashed twice and, according to his coach, "skated lousy." In 1977, Tickner won the nationals, but finished fifth in the world meet. He almost gave up the sport twice in 1978. Perhaps the problem with Charles Tickner has been that he skates so smoothly, he makes it look easy, and thus arouses little enthusiasm among the fans. This in turn influences the judges and their point totals.

Defending women's champion Linda Fratianne finished second in the 1978 World figure skating competition in Ottawa to East Germany's Anett Poetzsch, with the most exciting performance coming from the United States' Lisa-Marie Allen. Tai Babilonia and Randy Gardner, the first Americans to compete in the USSR are 1977-78 World bronze medalists and three-time national pair's champions. They have set their sights on capturing an Olympic gold medal, and have embarked on a rigorous training program, emphasizing stamina work, jogging, and running in parks. Randy has been weight lifting, and both engage in freestyle sessions daily, practice ballet, conditioning, and study jazz dance.

In men's competition at Lake Placid, Britain's John Curry, now a professional, is ineligible to defend his 1976 title at Innsbruck. Tickner or Robin Cousins of Britain is expected to fill the void left by Curry. Fratianne of Northridge, California, is a strong challenger for a gold in the women's. Babilonia and Gardner will be the United States' contenders for the gold in pairs.

Ice dancing was included for the first time in Olympic competition in 1976; the Russian pair of Ludmila Pakhomova and Sleksandr Gorschkov won the first Olympic gold medal awarded in the sport. The American team of O'Conner and Mills will return to Olympic competition at Lake Placid to challenge this strong Russian contingent.

ICE DANCING

1976	Ludmila Pakhomova & Aleksandr Gorschkov, USSR

MEN'S SINGLES

1908	Ulrich Sachow, Sweden
1920	Gillis Grafstrom, Sweden
1924	Gillis Grafstrom, Sweden
1928	Gillis Grafstrom, Sweden
1932	Karl Schaefer, Austria
1936	Karl Schaefer, Austria
1948	Richard T. Button, U.S.
1952	Richard T. Button, U.S.
1956	Hayes Alan Jenkins, U.S.
1960	David W. Jenkins, U.S.
1964	Manfred Schnelldorfer, Germany
1968	Wolfgang Schwartz, Austria
1972	Ondrej Nepela, Czechoslovakia
1976	John Curry, Great Britain

PAIRS

1908	Anna Hubler & Heinrich Burger, Germany
1920	Ludovika & Walter Jakobsson, Finland
1924	Helene Engelman & Alfred Berger, Austria
1928	Andree Joly & Pierre Brunet, France
1932	Andree Joly & Pierre Brunet, France
1936	Maxie Herber & Ernest Baier, Germany
1948	Micheline Lannoy & Pierre Baugniet, Belgium
1952	Ria and Paul Falk, Germany
1956	Elisabeth Schwarz & Kurt Oppelt, Austria
1960	Barbara Wagner & Robert Paul, Canada
1964	Ludmila Beloussova & Oleg Protopopov, USSR
1968	Ludmila Beloussova & Oleg Protopopov, USSR
1972	Irina Rodina & Alexei Ulanov, USSR
1976	Irina Rodina & Aleksandr Zaitzev, USSR

In 1961 a tragic airplane crash claimed the lives of all eighteen members of the United States figure skating team, shattering the high hopes for a strong American showing at the 1964 Olympics at Innsbruck, Austria. Many felt it would take at least a decade to develop new talent capable of competing at the world level. But no one had counted on the daughter of a *San Francisco Chronicle* pressman to emerge as one of the most charming and popular figure skating talents this country has known.

As Peggy Fleming began to show graceful promise as a skater, her father moved the family to Colorado where Peggy would have better facilities and receive proper coaching. The slender, beautiful brunette became dedicated to perfection. She practiced every spare moment to make the intricate maneuvers and difficult routines seem effortless. Peggy studied ballet to refine and modernize her routines to the background of compelling classical music. This was to become her style.

Peggy Fleming

At the age of fifteen, Peggy won the first of five consecutive national titles in 1964. She was selected to fill America's figure skating void at Innsbruck. She finished fifth. Deeply disappointed by her "failure," Peggy realized she would have to work much harder to improve the finer points of her performance.

In 1966, she won the first of her three World championships in Davos, Switzerland. After that victory, she set her sights on the Olympic gold medal in Grenoble, France in 1968. She repeated as World champion in 1967. In Grenoble, Peggy piled up an impressive lead during the first day of competition, then gracefully gliding, soaring, and spinning through a virtually flawless freestyle routine, she left the other competitors far behind. Peggy Fleming had captured the gold, and the hearts of many Americans, as she led the dramatic comeback of United States figure skating.

After taking her third World title, Peggy signed a lucrative contract to appear professionally in ice shows and television specials. Peggy's beautiful, imaginative performances elevated figure skating to an artistic, fascinating spectator sport.

WOMEN'S SINGLES

1908	Madge Syers, Great Britain
1920	Magda Julin-Mauroy, Sweden
1924	Mrs. Heima von Szabo-Planck, Austria
1928	Sonja Henie, Norway
1932	Sonja Henie, Norway
1936	Sonja Henie, Norway
1948	Barbara Ann Scott, Canada
1952	Jeanette Altwegg, Great Britain
1956	Tenley Albright, U.S.
1960	Carol Heiss, U.S.
1964	Sjoukje Dijkstra, Netherlands
1968	Peggy Fleming, U.S.
1972	Beatrix Schuba, Austria
1976	Dorothy Hamill, U.S.

CONTINENT

SPEED SKATING

STRONG SHOWING EXPECTED OF AMERICAN SKATERS

Historians generally agree that speed skating evolved on the canals of Holland around the middle of the thirteenth century, with the first competition taking place as early as 1676.

Skating was a way of life for the Dutch, whose towns and villages were interconnected with a network of frozen roads. On skates, everyone was brought within reach, and they could cover great distances "with a speed not exceeded by horses," as the poet Huig de Groot proudly wrote.

Among pioneering Dutch speed skating events, the first known women's competition was organized in 1805 on a straight course at Leeuwarden. Noted men's straight course races were held at Woutdsend in 1823, Dokkum in 1840, and Amsterdam in 1864. After this, tracks became U-shaped, with one sharp bend and an overall length of 160 to 200 meters (175 to 220 yards).

During the early nineteenth century, the Dutch took the sport to their neighbors, Germany, France, and Austria. The Frieslanders of North Holland introduced it to England in the area extending from Cambridge to the Wash known as the Fens, where recorded competitions date from 1814. *A Handbook of Fen Skating*, published in London in 1882, contained a drawing of a speed skating contest at Chatteris in 1823.

Among the earliest champions in the sport were William and George Smart, British professional skaters of the nineteenth century, who reigned for twenty years. Competition got underway in Norway in 1863, Sweden in 1882, Finland in 1883, and in Russia the following year. Speed skating came to North America in the mid-1800s; the earliest top calibre United States racer was Tim Donoghue, from 1863 to 1875. The first United States championships were held in 1879.

Norwegians who contributed generously to the popularity of speed skating internationally were Axel Paulsen, Harald Hagen, and Carl Werner. Rudolf Ericsson of Sweden was the first European men's champion, winning the title in Berlin in 1893. The first women's World title test was held in Stockholm in 1936 and was won by Kit Klein of the United States. Men's speed skating attained Olympic status in 1924; women's Olympic speed skating was added in 1960 at Squaw Valley, California.

The names of speed skating immortals have a decidedly foreign flavor. Among them are Oscar Mathisen of Norway, five times World champion; Clas Thunberg of Finland, who won five World titles and four Olympic gold medals; Ivar Ballangrud of Norway with four World titles and a like number of

The incomparable Eric Heiden sweeps to another speed skating title (preceding page). In World competition the last two years, Heiden has not lost a race, regardless of distance. Heiden's powerful legs and confident style may propel him to a record four gold medals at Lake Placid. Eric's sister Beth is expected to perform brilliantly for the women's team.

Olympic victories; and Hjalmar Andersen of Norway, three times World champion and the only male speed skater to win three gold medals in one Olympic meeting.

The most luminous women speed skaters have been Russian. They are Inga Artamonova, four times World title holder; Maria Isakova and Valentina Stenina, each World champion three times; and Lydia Skoblikova, who won six gold medals in two Winter Olympics, including all four in 1964.

The best American speed skaters competing today are: Eric and Beth Heiden, Mike Woods, Craig Kressler, Kim Kostron, Cindy Seikkula, Mary Docter, Dan Immerfall, Peter Mueller, Tom Plant, and Scott Guy. Leah Poulos-Mueller and Nancy Swider must also be included, as well as Sara Docter, Connie Paraskevin, and Steve Hickner. Unlike the European and Olympic style with two persons in each race, each staying in his own lane, most American races are "pack-style." Therefore, the American team must make special adjustments for Olympic competition.

In addition to the Russian women speed skaters, the East German duo of Christa Rothenburger and Sylvia Albrecht are expected to prove tough hurdles for Beth Heiden and her mates. Still the Heidens will be tough contenders for the Olympic gold medals in 1980. At least, that's how it looks to those objectively appraising the Olympic speed skating competition at Lake Placid. Not since the upset win of Terry McDermott in 1964 have Americans been in such favored position in an event once dominated by athletes representing the Scandinavian nations.

Eric Heiden, a premed student at the University of Wisconsin-Madison, just doesn't seem to lose in World competition, regardless of distance. His sprightly sister Beth propels herself almost as fast as her brother, and a lot faster than her female competitors in most events. Chances are good that the Heiden family will produce two World's champions and Olympic gold medal winners simultaneously in speed skating. In addition, Beth Heiden's teammate Leah Poulos-Mueller, a silver medalist in the 1976 Innsbruck Olympics, recently emerged from an eighteen-month hiatus to win the World sprint title for the second time.

Normally in speed skating and particularly in longer races, northern Europeans have surpassed other speed skaters because of their stamina and conditioning in cold climates. In the 1924 Olympics, Finland gained the three top spots in the 1,500, 5,000 and 10,000-meter races. In the shorter 500-meter race, Charles Jewtraw of the United States won the gold medal. In 1952, a Norwegian truck driver named Hjalmar Andersen won the first triple championship in speed skating since Ivar Ballangrud, also of Norway, in 1936. Andersen broke two World records and an Olympic record in the process. In more recent times, Russia has come to dominate speed skating competition—men's and women's. However, all this is likely to change drastically in 1980—courtesy of the Heiden family.

Last February at the Hague, Beth Heiden captured the World all-around title, winning all four events at distances from 500 to 3,000-meters. A week later Eric swept the World overall title for the third straight year, winning all four men's events—the 500, 1,500, 5,000, and 10,000-meter events—as well as setting a World record for total points. Eric went on to demolish competition in the sprints the following week, with sister Beth losing by an ice shaving or two, but already the all-round champion.

As in swimming, many observers believe speed skating events are so similar that, if rested, the same contestants would win any number of medals. The Wisconsin Heidens are out to prove that theory.

Although the Heiden brother-sister combination has attracted much of the pre-Olympic speed skating attention, another American pair may prove to be the Heiden's toughest competition at Lake Placid. Peter Mueller (right) and his wife, Leah Poulos-Mueller (below) are proven winners and an important part of the best speed skating team that has ever represented the United States or any other country. Peter captured the gold medal in the men's 1,000-meter at Innsbruck, and Leah won the silver in the women's 1,000-meter. The Muellers have been training extremely hard to give the Heidens a run for the gold at Lake Placid.

WOMEN'S EVENTS
500 METERS

1960	Helga Haase, Germany	0:45.9
1964	Lydia Skoblikova, USSR	0:45.0
1968	Ludmila Titova, USSR	0:46.1
1972	Anne Henning, U.S.	0:43.44
1976	Sheila Young, U.S.	0:42.76

1,000 METERS

1960	Klara Guseva, USSR	1:34.1
1964	Lydia Skoblikova, USSR	1:33.2
1968	Carolina Geijssen, Netherlands	1:32.6
1972	Monika Pflug, W. Germany	1:31..40
1976	Tatiana Averina, USSR	1:28.43

1,500 METERS

1960	Lydia Skoblikova, USSR	2:52.2
1964	Lydia Skoblikova, USSR	2:22.6
1968	Kaija Mustonen, Finland	2:22.4
1972	Dianne Holum, U.S.	2:20.85
1976	Galina Stepanskaya, USSR	2:16.58

3,000 METERS

1960	Lydia Skoblikova, USSR	5:14.3
1964	Lydia Skoblikova, USSR	5:14.9
1968	Johanna Schut, Netherlands	4:56.2
1972	Stien Baas-Kaiser, Netherlands	4:52.14
1976	Tatiana Averina, USSR	4:45.19

MEN'S EVENTS
500 METERS

1924	Charles Jewtraw, U.S.	0:44.0
1928	Clas Thunberg, Finland & Bernt Evensen, Norway (tie)	0:43.4
1932	John A. Shea, U.S.	0:43.4
1936	Ivar Ballangrud, Norway	0:43.4
1948	Finn Helgesen, Norway	0:43.1
1952	Kenneth Henry, U.S.	0:43.2
1956	Evgeniy Grishin, USSR	0:40.2
1960	Evgeniy Grishin, USSR	0:40.2
1964	Terry McDermott, U.S.	0:40.1
1968	Erhard Keller, W. Germany	0:40.3
1972	Erhard Keller, W. Germany	0:39.44

1976	Evgeny Kulikov, USSR	0:39.17

1,000 METERS

1976	Peter Mueller, U.S.	1:19.32

1,500 METERS

1924	Clas Thunberg, Finland	2:20.8
1928	Clas Thunberg, Finland	2:21.1
1932	John A. Shea, U.S.	2:57.2
1936	Charles Mathiesen, Norway	2:19.2
1948	Sverre Farstad, Norway	2:17.6
1952	Hjalmar Anderson, Norway	2:20.4
1956	Evgeniy Grishin, USSR	2:08.6
1960	Roald Edgar Aas, Norway &	
	Evgeniy Grishin, USSR (tie)	2:10.4
1964	Ants Anston, USSR	2:10.3
1968	Cornelis Verkerk, Netherlands	2:03.4
1972	Ard Schenk, Netherlands	2:02.96
1976	Jan Egil Storholt, Norway	1:59.38

5,000 METERS

1924	Clas Thunberg, Finland	8:39.0
1928	Ivar Ballangrud, Norway	8:50.5
1932	Irving Jaffee, U.S.	9:40.8
1936	Ivar Ballangrud, Norway	8:19.6
1948	Reidar Liakleb, Norway	8:29.4
1952	Hjalmar Anderson, Norway	8:10.6
1956	Boris Shilkov, USSR	7:48.7
1960	Viktor Kosichkin, USSR	7:51.3
1964	Knut Johannesen, Norway	7:38.4
1968	F. Anton Maier, Norway	7:22.4
1972	Ard Schenk, Netherlands	7:23.61
1976	Sten Stensen, Norway	7:24.48

10,000 METERS

1924	Julius Skutnabb, Finland	18:04.8
1928	Event not held, thawing of ice	
1932	Irving Jaffee, U.S.	19:13.6
1936	Ivar Ballangrud, Norway	17:24.3
1948	Ake Seyffarth, Norway	17:26.3
1952	Hjalmar Anderson, Norway	16:45.8
1956	Sigvard Ericsson, Sweden	16:35.9
1960	Knut Johannesen, Norway	15:46.6
1964	Jonny Nilsson, Sweden	15:50.1
1968	Jonny Hoeglin, Sweden	15:23.6
1972	Ard Schenk, Netherlands	15:01.3
1976	Piet Kleine, Netherlands	14:50.59

A GOLDEN PAIR

Speed skating is far and away the only winter Olympic event in which Americans have enjoyed continued success. And the speed skating team that will represent the United States at Lake Placid is the strongest ever. Competing on the team will be three medalists from the 1976 Olympics: Peter Mueller, gold medalist in the 1,000-meter, his wife, the former Leah Poulous, silver medalist in the women's 1,000-meter, and Dan Immerfall, winner of the bronze in the 500-meter. But defeating the perennial speed skating powers from Holland, Norway, and Russia will not be their primary objective. First, they must contend with two record shattering teammates, a phenomenal brother-sister combination from Madison, Wisconsin. If Eric and Beth Heiden can repeat their outstanding World championship performances, their fellow competitors will be vying for the silver and bronze medals at Lake Placid.

In 1978, at the World junior championships in Montreal, Beth and Eric each competed in four events. The results were astonishing. They swept every event, each winning four gold medals. Never before had any individual swept all four events in that competition.

Tiny Beth Heiden zips around the speed skating oval in pursuit of a sparkling performance at the Olympics in 1980 (left). Eric and Beth flash the smiles which just might be seen repeatedly from the gold medal stand at the awards ceremonies at Lake Placid, if both can continue their recent phenomenal success in the Olympics (above).

That a brother and sister both did is truly remarkable.

The 1978 women's sprint championships were held at the recently completed Olympic rink at Lake Placid. Beth, at 5′1″ and 99 pounds, offered a startling contrast to the classic, massive bodies of the world's finest speed skaters. It seemed impossible that this tiny woman could threaten these powerful skaters. But what Beth lacks in size and strength, she more than makes up for with intelligence, form, and a style of skating that permits her to achieve maximum efficiency with every stroke. Beth did very well, finishing second overall to Liubov Sadchikova of Russia. On February 4, 1979 she won the World all-around championship by sweeping all four events. In the World sprint championships at Inzell, Beth handled Sadchikova with no problem, but Leah Poulos-Mueller won the overall title returning from an eighteen-month layoff.

At nineteen, Beth is a sophomore at the University of Wisconsin-Madison, majoring in civil engineering. She is very bright, but small in stature for a speed skater. By constantly refining her form to develop better efficiency, she compensates for her size. Her other interests are diving, running, and cycling; her burning desire to win and total dedication to sports is equaled only by that of her brother.

The world is fairly well-acquainted with the incredible success of Eric Heiden. When he was seventeen, Eric finished nineteenth at the Olympics in the 5,000-meter race at Innsbruck in 1976. Since that relatively uneventful day, Eric simply does not lose anymore in World competition, regardless of distance. Coaches, competitors, and admirers all predict Eric will be the best speed skater of all-time, if not already.

In the 1977 men's World championships in Heerenveen, Netherlands, Eric became the first American to win the overall title in the 76-year history of the event. In the same year he won the World sprint championships and the World junior championship. In 1978 he repeated as champion in all three races. On February 11, 1979 in Oslo, Norway, Eric exploded to his third consecutive overall World title by again winning all four events. His point total established a new world record. At the races at Inzell, Eric took the 500, 1,500, and 5,000-meter with his usual, powerful flair, clinching his eighth World championship in eight attempts. But in the 10,000-meter, with the championship already in his possession, Eric put on an awesome display of burning intensity; he sliced seven seconds off the stadium record. In a sport where a fraction of a second is usually the difference between racers, Eric finished the 6¼ miles an incredible 15.64 seconds in front of the second place racer. Eric is on top of the world.

Much of the Heiden success can be attributed to Diane Holum, the only woman coach of World class speed skaters. Holum was a great skater in her own right, having won a silver and a bronze medal in the 1968 Olympics, and a gold and silver in 1972. That year she moved to Madison from Northbrook, Illinois, and agreed to coach at the local speed skating club where Eric and Beth were members.

The Heidens were placed on a unique training program, stressing dry land training of all varieties; bicycling, weight lifting and special exercises devised by Holum to imitate proper skating technique. Eric also plays soccer for the University of Wisconsin. Beth and Eric worked extremely hard. They drove the tiresome seventy-five miles to the West Allis Olympic rink every day to work out for a minimum of four-and-a-half hours. Nothing comes easy in speed skating.

If Holum had not moved to Madison, Eric would probably be playing right wing for the Badger hockey team. Since Eric was three, he has loved skating. He began playing hockey at five. He has always been fast, but his only racing experience was pack-style racing, which is similar to a strategic distance race in track. At sixteen hockey was still Eric's first love, but that year he received an invitation to Europe to compete in the World junior championships. It was then he decided to concentrate on speed skating. Two years later, he was the best in the world.

Eric, twenty-one, has postponed his pre-med studies at the University of Wisconsin-Madison until after the Olympics, so he can give even more of his time to speed skating. He is already in a class of his own due to hard work, determination, and the high level of self-confidence that comes from consistent winning. There will be five men's speed skating events at Lake Placid; and Eric Heiden will probably come home with five gold medals.

Following are some of Eric Heiden's thoughts as he prepares for the Olympics. The quotes are printed with permission from the *Milwaukee Sentinel*.

"Skating takes up all of my time. It is my

whole life right now. But I wouldn't give it up for anyone or anything. I am looking forward to it all ending. There are things that I have wanted to do that the longer I stay away from them, the more I wish I could do them. There have been a lot of sacrifices. When you first get into something, you notice the missing things the most. The biggest thing I missed was playing hockey. I just sort of dropped it.

"People will think that I don't have any fun. It may sound hard, but it doesn't seem that way to me. If I weren't getting anywhere, it wouldn't be fun. But I am getting somewhere.

"For me, I think I lead a pretty normal life. But then, this is the only life I have known. Others say that I miss a lot of social life, but if you've got to be at the ice rink at 8 A.M. Saturday morning, that means getting up at 5 A.M. You can't stay up late on Friday night.

"I am at the point where I have put in so much time that I can't slack off. Oh, I have bagged a workout or two, but I usually get mad at myself for doing it. And there have been times when I have really gotten tired of it.

"You know, it's an awesome feeling knowing you're the best in the world at something. It all happened so suddenly. In the '76 Olympics I was seventh in one event and nineteenth in the other, and I thought things would never click.

"But then I won the World's two years ago, and I just had to keep going. I was sure it was a fluke. I had to prove to myself and everybody else that I won fair and square. And then I won the World's again last year. What keeps me going is personal satisfaction. It used to be encouragement from my parents and coach, but now it is something from within me, something that is in my heart.

"It's funny, even though I win a lot, I am not always happy. If I win and don't skate a good time, I am very upset. I always want to give my all. I put a lot of pressure on myself to do well. I am a serious person and very competitive.

"I've got to do it all now, because when I get older, it will be too late. I don't ever want to look back and be sorry that I didn't do everything I could."

The most remarkable performance in Winter Olympic history belongs to Lydia Skobilikova. She swept all four women's speed skating gold medals in the 1964 Olympics at Innsbruck, Austria, becoming the only person to ever win four gold medals in one Winter Olympics. The compact Russian school teacher won two gold medals four years earlier at Squaw Valley in her first Olympic appearance. She is the most outstanding individual performer in Olympic speed skating history.

BOBSLED

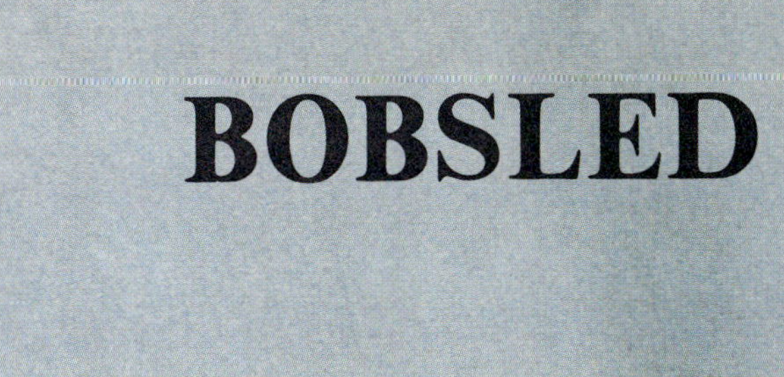

NEW COURSE MAY HELP FUTURE AMERICAN SLEDDERS

Bobsledding is called "the champagne of thrills"—and rightly so. Aboard a modern bobsled, with streamlined cowl-and-wheel steering, two-man and four-man teams reach speeds of almost ninety miles-per-hour. To ride a veritable ice rocket down frozen mountain slopes, where a slight slip can cause terminal disaster, is a feat for only the most daring.

While no one can speak with empirical knowledge, evidence suggests that the original "bobsled" may have been created to transport large animal carcasses home for food—such as the Indians of North America did on their toboggans. The toboggan is the forerunner of the modern bobsled. After a time, it was discovered that if the wooden toboggan were mounted on runners, far greater speeds could be attained; but the danger also increased, because the higher center of gravity made the vehicle more difficult to control. In 1885, a newer, heavier sled with added ballast was developed. This helped keep the manned trajectory on course—it was also faster and safer. The new sleds were called "bobsleighs," because their riders would "bob" to increase speeds on a straightway, which required perfect unison by the team to be effective.

Bobsledders eventually laid out their own course, the famous and dangerous Cresta Run in the Swiss Alps. New features on sleds permitted them to go even faster; soon the Cresta Run became too dangerous, and an artificial run was built in St. Moritz. By 1917, there were some one hundred bobsled courses in Europe. National championships began and by 1924, when the winter games became part of the Olympic program, bobsledders conducted their first international race. It was won by a four-man Swiss team.

Americans obtained permission to represent their country in the 1928 Olympics and won the competition that year, which signified the beginnings of repeated United States victories in the sport. By the time of the 1932 Olympics, Americans had developed many innovations on the equipment used and swept the competition that year. American dominance in bobsledding continued for many years, with the United States spearheading changes and refinements. Courses also changed; today bobsled tracks are permanently constructed concrete foundations over which snow and water are frozen to make a glare ice surface.

Olympic bobsledding events are divided into two categories: the four-man bob and the two-man bob. Since 1948 Europeans have dominated competition, with the East Germans, Swiss, and Austrians fielding the strongest teams. The international press alludes to world class bobsledding teams as the "big four." The East Germans have two powerful crews headed by Meinhard Nehmer, the 1976 Olympic gold medalist in both two and four-man sleds, and teammate Horst Schonau. The Swiss team is next, led by Erich Scharer, a bronze and silver medal winner in two and four-man competition. Behind them loom the West Germans and

The Japanese two-man bobsled team carefully maneuvers their craft through the icy twists and turns on the harrowing bobsled run at Innsbruck (preceding page). The newly constructed run at Lake Placid should prove equally thrilling.

Austrians. Reasons given for the preeminence of the "big four" center on training time and facilities available to sledders. While most of them must rely on winter cold for ice tracks, the Austrians, for instance, have a new refrigerated run at Innsbruck. They begin training in late October and work out every night during winter. The West Germans have a refrigerated track at Konigssee, and the East Germans have a course at Oberhof. The Swiss have their track at St. Moritz, and frequently travel to Innsbruck or Konigssee to train when St. Moritz is down.

United States sledders could not begin training until mid-January, and had little time to polish their techniques. Now the Mount Van Hoevenberg run at Lake Placid, which was used in the 1932 Olympics, has been replaced by a new $2.9 million refrigerated course. Hopefully this will help the Americans become a factor in international bobsledding circles once again, although it is too late to help in the 1980 Winter Olympics. Having a new course in their "own backyard" should prove a boon to United States sledders in future Olympic years. Meanwhile, Marine Paul Vincent and his American mates will do their best at Lake Placid.

4-MAN BOB
(Driver in parentheses)

1924	Switzerland (Edward Scherrer)	5:45.54
1928	*United States (William Fiske) (A)	3:20.5
1932	United States (William Fiske)	7:53.68
1936	Switzerland (Pierre Musy)	5:19.85
1948	United States (Edward Rimkus)	5:20.1
1952	Germany (Andreas Ostler)	5:07.84
1956	Switzerland (Frank Kapus)	5:10.44
1964	Canada (Victor Emery)	4:14.46
1968	Italy (Eugenio Monti) (A)	2:17.39
1972	Switzerland (Jean Wicki)	4:43.07
1976	E. Germany (Meinhard Nehmer)	3:40.43
	*Five-Man Bobsled (A) 2 races	

2-MAN BOB

1932	United States (Hubert Stevens)	8:14.74
1936	United States (Ivan Brown)	5:29.29
1948	Switzerland (F. Enrich)	5:29.2
1952	Germany (Andreas Ostler)	5:24.54
1956	Italy (Dalla Costa)	5:30.14
1964	Great Britain (Antony Nash)	4:21.90
1968	Italy (Eugenio Monti)	4:41.54
1972	W. Germany (Wolfgang Zimmerer)	4:47.07
1976	E. Germany (Meinhard Nehmer)	3:40.43

BIATHLON

NOT MUCH HOPE FOR A MEDAL

The Biathlon, added to the Winter Olympics in 1960, combines shooting and skiing and had long been popular in Scandinavian countries where it had obvious military value.

The Biathlon is a ski race of approximately twelve and one-half miles, broken by four shooting events. The skier arrives at an established range, takes his position on a numbered firing point, and fires five shots at a target with a corresponding number. The target is not marked until after each shooter has left the range. Scoring for this event is really a hit-or-miss proposition. A miss adds *two minutes* to the total elapsed course time, with the winner chosen on the basis of the least elapsed corrected time. Ranges differ, target sizes differ, and two shooting positions are required—standing and prone.

The Biathlon is a tough, demanding event, requiring endurance and a combination of completely different skills. After a competitor has skied miles at top speed, he arrives at the first rifle range. He flops down in the snow, gets off his five shots, climbs back up, and takes off for more miles to the next target area. Here he encounters a different length range and a different size target. When he gets there, he is undoubtedly winded and puffing, a poor condition for careful, accurate shooting. Since his hits are *not* marked as he shoots, he has no idea if he is close to the bulls-eye or errant. His rifle sights may be frozen; his glasses may be steamed; he must estimate wind conditions as he goes. What he calculates as "on target" for one range has no relation to adjustments he must make for the next.

A biathlete rushes to the next target area to compete in the shooting segment of the event (preceding page). Competitors in the biathlon must combine cross-country skiing strength and stamina with accurate marksmanship to win the grueling event. The United States has never come close to doing well in either biathlon event.

The choice of rifle is left to the contestant, but he must carry it twelve-and-a-half miles as well as shoot with it, so it must be light and wieldy. Results indicate that rifle shooting is as important in this event as skiing prowess. In the first Biathlon, only one man made twenty hits with his twenty shots. Klas Lestander of Sweden had an elapsed "corrected" time of 1 hour, 33 minutes, 21.6 seconds. Tryvainen of Finland finished second with a corrected time of 1 hour, 33 minutes, 57.7 seconds; he had missed two shots, and four minutes penalty time had been added to his finish time. The fastest *skier* did *not* win the event—the best *shooter* did! In the first event, there was a difference of approximately fifteen minutes in skiing time registered—in the same group, penalty points added for poor shooting varied from zero to thirty-six minutes. Ironically, France's Arben had both the shortest skiing time *and* the most penalty points, ending up in twenty-fifth place.

The best United States finish in 1964 was sixteenth—far behind Vladimir Melanin of the USSR. In 1972, in Sapporo, Japan, Magnar Solberg of Norway took the gold medal, repeating his 1968 victory. The best United States finish was fourteenth. Lack of training facilities and a general lack of interest accounts for the poor showing of the United States in the Biathlon event.

A "relay" has been added, but United States chances for a medal in the 1980 Olympic games are remote. The United States will field a team; but it will do well to improve on its eleventh place finish (out of fifteen teams in relay) and even less admirable past showing in individual competition.

A biathlete prepares to drop into position to join his fellow competitors in the shooting segment of the biathlon. An accurate target score is as important as a strong skiing performance in this interesting and unfamiliar sport.

BIATHLON (20 km.)

1960	Klas Lestander, Sweden	1:33:21.6
1964	Vladimir Melanin, USSR	1:20:26.8
1968	Magnar Solberg, Norway	1:13:45.9
1972	Magnar Solberg, Norway	1:15:55.50
1976	Nikolai Kruglov, USSR	1:14:12.26

BIATHLON RELAY (40 km.)

1968	USSR, Norway, Sweden	2:13.02
1972	USSR, Finland, E. Germany	1:51.44
1976	USSR, Finland, E. Germany	1:57.55.64

CROSS-COUNTRY SKIING

SERIOUS COMPETITORS AT LAST

When Norwegian Sondre Nordheim, outfitted in ski bindings he invented, traversed a distance of 115 miles to Oslo from Morgedal, Telemark, international competitive cross-country skiing was born.

Cross-country, or Nordic ski racing, is the oldest form of competitive skiing; its ancestry is part of Norwegian history. Races had taken place since 1767; but after Nordheim designed his ski gear in the 1880s, the sport was introduced to every continent.

Peak fitness and dedicated training are essential to the successful Nordic skier. A long, rhythmic stride, with emphasis on the bent front knee and a full arm swing, controls the basic pendulum action. Turns are made by a relatively simple skating movement, shifting the weight to the inside ski. The art of using ski poles for added thrust is an important technique; the cross-country skier gradually learns to transform every stride into an energy-conserving movement.

A cross-country course consists of varying sections of uphill, downhill, and flat terrain. Artificial obstacles are not permitted. In world and Olympic championships, competitors start at half-minute intervals, with each participant being timed to the nearest tenth of a second. Outstanding Olympic performers in the past have been those representing Sweden, Finland, and Norway. Sweden's Sixten Jernberg and Finland's Veikko Hakulinen are names that remain revered in the sport.

A lone cross-country skier takes long strides to try to cover the scenic course in the best time (preceding page).

Men's races are contested over 15, 30, and 50-kilometer distances, the equivalent to 9.3, 18.6, and 31 miles. Women's distances are 5 and 10-kilometers, corresponding to 3.1 and 6.2 miles. Women's events, added to the Olympic program in 1964, have brought Russian women to the forefront of cross-country competition. Relay races incorporate four times 10-kilometers for men, three times 5-kilometers for women.

Until 1976, no American had ever won a medal in Nordic skiing. The best the United States had done was a fifteenth place finish in 1932 at Lake Placid. In 1976, Billy Koch appeared on the scene and won a silver medal in the 30-kilometer cross-country event at Innsbruck. The twenty-year-old Koch immediately became famous; he had beaten every famed racer from Europe and Scandinavia, except for Sergei Saveliev, an experienced Russian. Koch, a Vermont native, achieved his deed despite chronic asthma. After his Olympic "near-victory," Koch was beseiged by numerous pressures and decided to quit racing. Reconsidering his decision, Koch participated in the world championships in Finland last February, and placed fifteenth in the 15-kilometer event and thirty-third in the 30-kilometer. Since that time, Koch has come on strong, building his endurance and techniques, hoping to peak at the 1980 Olympics.

Another contender among the American Nordic Skiing team is Alison Owen-Spencer, a twenty-five-year-old from Anchorage, Alaska. She is the first American woman ever to win a World Cup Cross-Country race, and completed the last season in seventh place in World Cup standings, behind five Russians and one Norwegian.

The American team has served notice that it has the individual talent necessary to be highly competitive in 1980.

MEN'S CROSS-COUNTRY EVENTS

15 KILOMETERS (9.3 miles) OR EQUIVALENT

1924	Thorleif Haug, Norway	1:14:31
1928	Johan Grottumsbraaten, Norway	1:37:01
1932	Sven Utterstrom, Sweden	1:23:07
1936	Erik-August Larsson, Sweden	1:14:38
1948	Martin Lundstrom, Sweden	1:13:50
1952	Hallgeir Brenden, Norway	1:01:34
1956	Hallgeir Brenden, Norway	49:39.0
1960	Haakon Brusveen, Norway	51:55.0
1964	Eero Mantyranta, Finland	50:54.1
1968	Harald Groenningen, Norway	47:54.2
1972	Sven-Ake Lundback, Sweden	45:28.24
1976	Nikolai Bajukov, USSR	43:58.47

(Note:approx. 18-kilometer course 1924-1952)

30 KILOMETERS (18.6 miles)

1956	Veikko Hakulinen, Finland	1:44:06.0
1960	Sixten Jernberg, Sweden	1:51:03.9
1964	Eero Mantyranta, Finland	1:30:50.7
1968	Franco Nones, Italy	1:35:39.2
1972	Vyacheslav Vedenin,USSR	1:36:31.1
1976	Sergei Savaliev, USSR	1:30:29.38

50 KILOMETERS (31 miles)

1924	Thorleif Haug, Norway	3:44:32.0
1928	Per Erik Hedlund, Sweden	4:52:03.0
1932	Veli Saarinen, Finland	4:28:00.0
1936	Elis Viklund, Sweden	3:30:11.0
1948	Nils Karlsson, Sweden	3:47:48.0
1952	Veikko Hakulinen, Finland	3:33:33.0
1956	Sixten Jernberg, Sweden	2:50:27.0
1960	Kalevi Hamalainen, Finland	2:59:06.3
1964	Sixten Jernberg, Sweden	2:43:52.6
1968	Ole Ellefsaeter, Norway	2:28:45.8
1972	Paal Tyldum, Norway	2:43:14.7
1976	Ivar Formo, Norway	2:37:30.05

40-KILOMETER CROSS-COUNTRY RELAY

1936	Finland, Norway, Sweden	2:41:33.0
1948	Sweden, Finland, Norway	2:32:08.0
1952	Finland, Norway, Sweden	2:20:16.0
1956	USSR, Finland, Sweden	2:15:30.0
1960	Finland, Norway, USSR	2:18:45.6
1964	Sweden, Finland, USSR	2:18:34.6
1968	Norway, Sweden, Finland	2:08:33.5
1972	USSR, Norway, Switzerland	2:04:47.94
1976	Finland, Norway, USSR	2:07:59.72

60
BIATHLON
華民國

A Japanese biathlete competes in the cross-country skiing segment of the biathlon. After skiing several miles, the competitors arrive at a target area where they exchange their ski poles for the rifle on their backs. At the target site competitors rely on shooting accuracy to win additional points. A biathlete is a unique individual in that he must possess the strength and stamina of a cross-country skier and the exacting eye of a marksman.

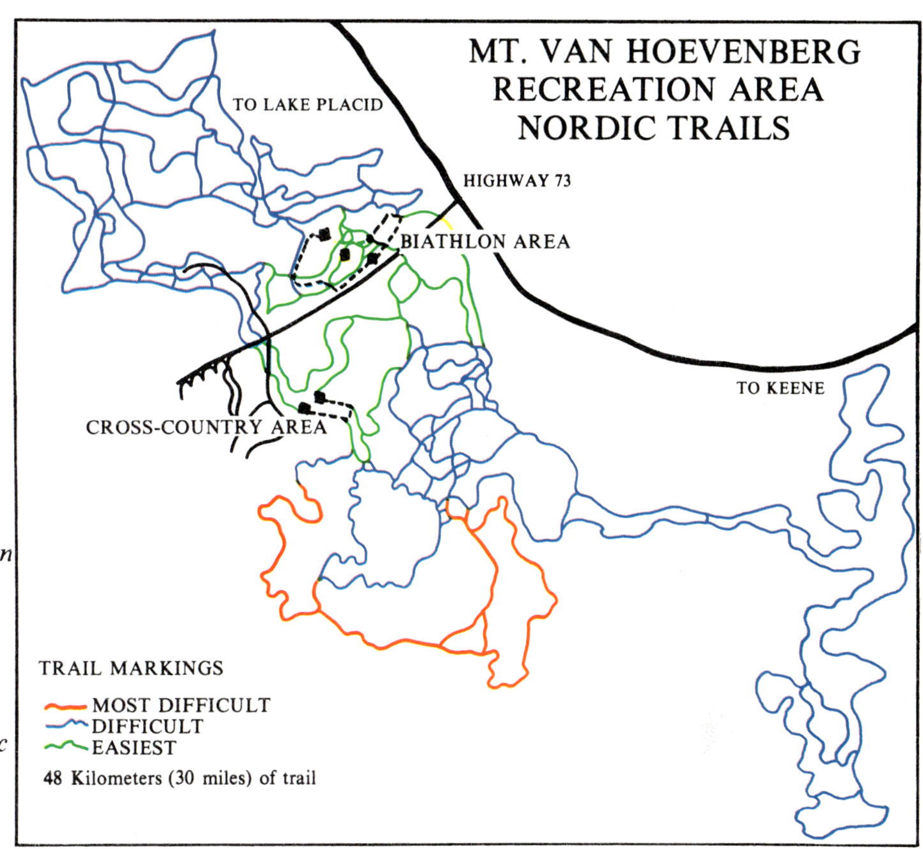

The state-owned Mt. Van Hoevenberg Recreation Area is the site for four Olympic sports: bobsledding, luge, biathlon, and cross-country skiing. The complex loop of ski touring trails (see map at right) is on the edge of the scenic High Peaks Wilderness Area in New York's beautiful Adirondack Mountains. When Olympic racers are not competing on the system of secluded trails, all are open to the public at no cost.

WOMEN'S CROSS-COUNTRY EVENTS

5 KILOMETERS (approx. 3.1 miles)

1964	Claudia Boyarskikh, USSR	17:50.5
1968	Toini Gustafsson, Sweden	16:45.2
1972	Galina Koulacova, USSR	17:00.5
1976	Helena Takalo, Finland	15:48.69

10 KILOMETERS (6.2 miles)

1952	Lydia Wideman, Finland	41:40.0
1956	Lyubov Kosyreva, USSR	38:11.0
1960	Maria Gusakova, USSR	39:46.6
1964	Claudia Boyarskikh, USSR	40:24.3
1968	Toini Gustafsson, Sweden	36:46.5
1972	Galina Koulacova, USSR	34:17.82
1976	Raisa Smetanina, USSR	30:13.41

15-KILOMETER CROSS-COUNTRY RELAY

1956	Finland, USSR, Sweden	1:09:01.0
1960	Sweden, USSR, Finland	1:04:21.4
1964	USSR, Sweden, Finland	59:20.2
1968	Norway, Sweden, USSR	57:30.0
1972	USSR, Finland, Norway	48:46.1
1976	USSR, Finland, E. Germany (20 km. in 1976)	1:07:49.75

AMERICA'S FIRST MEDALIST

In the 1976 Winter Olympics at Innsbruck, Bill Koch emerged as America's first world class competitor by winning a silver medal in the 30-kilometer cross-country skiing event. Koch's surprising finish made him the first American to win a medal in an Olympic cross-country event. The best U.S. finish at an Olympics had been fifteenth place at Lake Placid in 1932.

Koch had beaten all of the famed racers from Eastern Europe and Scandanavia. Only Sergei Saveliev, a Russian, covered the course faster. With Koch's remarkable victory, the United States Nordic Ski Team finally achieved international prominence. The twenty-year-old champion from Guilford, Vermont became the toast of the skiing world. Koch was surrounded by admirers and reporters. More triumphs and greater things were expected of Bill Koch.

After finishing a very disappointing twenty-seventh in his first race of the 1977 season at Telemark, Wisconsin, Koch was fed up with all the outside pressure placed on him. He quit skiing and returned home to devote more time to his wife Katie and their newborn daughter. "There was pressure from all directions," Koch told *Sports Illustrated,* "Everybody wanted me to win. Skiing has to be enjoyable or you can't be successful. And after the Olympics it wasn't enjoyable anymore."

After competing on the 1972 and 1976 Olympic teams, it did not seem likely that Koch would compete in the 1980 Winter Games; but Koch returned to racing last year. He was hampered early in the season by bronchitis and chronic asthma, a major obstacle for a man in his sport. Koch turned things around at the Federation International Ski world championships at Lahti, Finland, last February. He was the best United States finisher in the 15-kilometer and 30-kilometer events, placing fifteenth and thirty-third respectively. Following the championships, Koch regained his strength and peace of mind. In three races in Sweden, Koch skied stride for stride with the top five European finishers in the early going. He won the night race at Ostersund and finished thirteenth in the 30-kilometer event at Falun.

With an additional year of serious training, Koch feels he can regain the level of endurance required to compete with the European skiers at Lake Placid in 1980. Koch has been seriously training since he was thirteen. Now, ten years later, he is ready to lead the United States Nordic Ski Team into the Winter Olympics for the second time.

The new Nordic World Cup season opened at Telemark in February, and Koch was ready. He placed sixth in the 15-kilometer event, one minute behind the surprise winner Ove Aunli of Norway. Koch finished ahead of world champion Sven-Ake Lundback of Sweden and just a fraction of a second behind the other world champion Josef Luszczeck of Poland. It was Koch's best performance since Innsbruck. The United States is ready to be taken seriously in Olympic Nordic ski racing in 1980, thanks largely to the efforts of America's premier cross-country skier, Bill Koch.

Prior to the 1976 Olympics, America never had a medalist in a cross-country skiing event. At Innsbruck, American Bill Koch raced across the 30-kilometer course fast enough to finish a very surprising second (right). Sergi Saveliev of Russia covered the course in world record time . . . only eighteen seconds ahead of Koch. Koch is a member of the United States Nordic Ski Team to compete at Lake Placid.

7

SKI JUMPING

SOARING TO VICTORY

Courage, grace, style, and form, as well as leaping distance, combine to make the Olympic ski jumping event picturesque, thrilling, and exacting. Ski jumping is probably the most spectacular of spectator sports, blending speed and power with the application of basic flight principles.

In Olympic ski jumping, the man who jumps the farthest does not necessarily win. Points are awarded for style, posture, and technique. The competitor is given pluses or minuses based on an assortment of factors, only one being the total distance covered. Elements influencing the jumper's final total points include whether the jumper reduces speed on his way down the ramp, whether his launching "spring" is properly timed as he takes off and soars into the air; his posture of straight knees, an extreme forward lean from the ankles with just a light curve of hips and back, whether his skis are parallel and, during the landing pattern, whether his skis are inclined slightly upwards.

Faults are penalized, such as an unsteady or oblique position of the body or arms, a curved or hollow back, bent knees, or unsteady skis. At "touchdown," the seconds just previous to landing, the ski jumper moves one foot forward with knees bent to absorb the shock. Stiffness or unsteadiness at this time results in a loss of points. If the skier touches the snow-covered ground with any part of his body during landing, he is also penalized.

The International Ski Federation and the Olympic Committee set precise standards for ski jumps—the newly constructed jump at Intervale meets these specifications in every way. In Olympic and World Championship competition, athletes perform on 70 and 90-meter ski jumps. The size of any ski jump is determined by the distance along the ground from the point of take-off to an engineering point on the landing known as the "norm" point, approximately two-thirds of the way to the point where landing begins. The distance from the edge of the jump to the take-off platform is 83 meters (270 feet) and the slope is 33 degrees. The first Olympic and World championships were won by Jacob Tullin-Thams of Norway in 1924. Only one all-jumping event continued in Olympic competition until 1964, when 90-meter and 70-meter jumps were introduced. The 1980 Olympic ski jumping events will be held at Intervale, just a mile and a half outside of Lake Placid. Designers felt it was important to build ski jumping facilities on the nearest possible location, because of the huge spectator crowds attracted.

Jim Denney, America's premier ski jumper, soars through the air with perfect form (preceding page). Form and style count as heavily as distance in judging the event. With a good day at Lake Placid, Denney could become America's first ski jumping medalist.

When conditions are right, and every conceivable effort is made to perfect them in Olympic competition, ski jumping is a relatively safe sport and the incidence of injury is small. Contrary to how it may appear on television, jumpers are usually not more than ten feet in the air at any time, as their flight curve follows that of the descending hill. In the event of a fall, the skier normally slides down the landing area until he skids to a halt on the flat.

Ski jumping equipment has been drastically affected by technological changes. The skis themselves measure from 240 to 255 centimeters in length and half-again as wide as the Alpine ski. Each ski weighs from twelve to fifteen pounds, and is similar in construction to Alpine skis. The skis are constructed from a combination of wood, fiber glass, epoxy, and a p-tex bottom, which contains five or six narrow grooves to help run straight in the tracks and on the landing. Jumping ski boots are similar to the older model Alpine leather boots, with a flexible sole and a high back. The binding permits the heel to move freely up and down when in

SKI JUMPING (90 meters)

1924	Jacob T. Thams, Norway	227.5
1928	Alfred Andersen, Norway	230.5
1932	Birger Ruud, Norway	228.0
1936	Birger Ruud, Norway	232.0
1948	Petter Hugsted, Norway	228.1
1952	A. Bergmann, Norway	226.0
1956	Antti Hyvarinen, Finland	227.0
1960	Helmut Recknagel, Germany	227.2
1964	Toralf Engan, Norway	230.7
1968	Vladimir Beloussov, USSR	231.3
1972	Wojiech Fortuna, Poland	219.9
1976	Karl Schnabl, Austria	234.8

SKI JUMPING (70 meters)

1964	Veikko Kankkonen, Finland	229.9
1968	Jiri Raska, Czechoslovakia	216.5
1972	Yukio Kasaya, Japan	244.2
1976	Hans Aschenbach, E. Germany	252.0

15-KILOMETER CROSS-COUNTRY & JUMPING

1924	Thorleif Haug, Norway	453.800
1928	Johan Grottumsbraaten, Norway	427.800
1932	Johan Grottumsbraaten, Norway	446.200
1936	Oddbjom Hagen, Norway	430.300
1948	Heikki Hasu, Finland	448.800
1952	Simon Slattvik, Norway	451.621
1956	Sverre Stenersen, Norway	455.000
1960	Georg Thoma, Germany	457.952
1964	Tormod Knutsen, Norway	469.280
1968	Franz Keller, W. Germany	449.040
1972	Ulrich Wehling, E. Germany	413.340
1976	Ulrich Wehing, E. Germany	423.390

the air. Suits worn by ski jumpers also help determine the aerodynamic soundness of a skier's airflight position, for without proper fit, the skier will lose a portion of "lift" effect. All ski jumpers are required to wear protective helmets.

Ski jumpers generally train year-round. They practice building strength in their legs by gymnastics and agility work to improve balance and air sensitivity, speed training to improve reflexes, and on a variety of devices such as roller-ski jumps and take-off machines.

In 1980, the United States will pin its hopes on the members of the U.S. jumping team: Jim and Jeff Denney, Terry Kern, Steve Haik, Chris McNeill, Jeff Davis, John Broman, John Bassette and Kip Sundgaard. At twenty-two, Jim Denney of Duluth, Minnesota, has emerged as the best United States jumper competing in international competition in more than a decade. He began jumping at age four in his backyard; the oldest of four boys, three have followed in his ski tracks. Jon Denney is a member of the U.S. Junior squad. Chris McNeill of

Polaris, Montana, had his best year as an international skier in 1978, registering a number of wins in top competition.

The most successful international ski jumper has been Birger Ruud of Norway, with five World and two Olympic titles to his credit. Norway continues to beget the greatest number of outstanding jumpers. Art Devlin, four-time United States ski jump champion, three-time North American champion, and a member of the United States Ski Hall of Fame, is a Lake Placid resident, who has spent many hours jumping at Intervale. Devlin, a former member of the United States Olympic ski jumping team, said recently: "In my opinion, before they ever built the new hills, the 70-meter hill was the best in the world." He added that the new jumps are excellent, and their proximity to the Lake Placid location represents a tremendous asset for the event.

A ski jumper leans out over his skis, to reach for all the distance he can, as he takes off over Innsbruck in the 1976 Olympics. Before he gracefully touches down (on the white surface partially visible at the bottom of the photo), he will have traveled 200 to 250 meters through the air. Ski jumping will be a thrilling favorite among the thousands of spectators, who will line the newly constructed ski towers at Intervale near Lake Placid.

Ulrich Wehling soars off the 70-meter ski jump enroute to victory and an Olympic gold medal in the Nordic combined event during the 1972 Winter Games at Sapporo. Wehling, a nineteen-year-old East German high school student at the time, is the only person to win two Nordic combined events. He repeated his feat at the 1976 Olympics at Innsbruck. Upon completion of a 15-kilometer cross-country ski race, Nordic combined athletes move to the 70-meter jump for the second half of the event. Points are awarded for each segment of the event with the highest combined point total winning the gold.

THE CLOSING CEREMONY

In the closing ceremony, which takes place in the stadium after the last event has been completed, flagbearers of participating delegations march into the arena in single file behind their shield bearers in the same order as during the Opening Ceremony. Behind them march six competitors from each delegation which has participated in the Games, eight or ten abreast, without distinction of nationality, uniting all in the friendly bonds of Olympic sport. Flagbearers form a semicircle behind the rostrum.

The President of the International Olympic Committee proceeds to the foot of the rostrum, where the Greek national anthem accompanies the raising of the Greek flag on the *right* flagpole, also used for individual victory ceremonies. The flag of the country organizing the Games is hoisted on the *center* flagpole while its national anthem is played. Finally, the flag of the country selected to organize the next Olympic Games is hoisted on the *left* flagpole as its national anthem is played. In an official proclamation from the rostrum, the President of the International Olympic Committee pronounces the closing of the Games and calls upon the youth of all nations to participate in the next Olympic Games, four years hence.

A fanfare is sounded and the sacred Olympic Fire is extinguished. As the Olympic Anthem is played, the Olympic Flag is slowly lowered and carried horizontally from the arena by a squad of eight men in uniform. A five-gun salute follows, a choir sings, then standard bearers, flag carriers, and competitors march out to appropriate music played by all the assembled bands.

Schedule continued from page 5

SUNDAY, FEB. 17

Figure Skating: ice dance, compulsory dance, and original set pattern—
Olympic Center 14:00
pairs free skating—Olympic Center 19:30
Speed Skating: women's 1,000-meter—Olympic Oval 10:30
Alpine Skiing: women's downhill—Whiteface Mountain 11:30
Ski Jumping: 70-meter special—Intervale 13:00
Cross-Country Skiing: men's special 15-kilometer—Mt. Van Hoevenberg........ 09:00
Awards Ceremonies—Mirror Lake........ 19:30

MONDAY, FEB. 18

Figure Skating: men's compulsory figures—Olympic Center 08:00
Alpine Skiing: men's giant slalom 1st run—Whiteface Mountain 10:00
Ski Jumping: 70-meter combined—Intervale........ 12:30
Cross-Country Skiing: women's 10-kilometer—Mt. Van Hoevenberg 09:00
Ice Hockey—Olympic Center (two rinks) 13:00-13:30
16:30-17:00
20:00-20:30
Awards Ceremonies—Mirror Lake........ 19:30

TUESDAY, FEB. 19

Figure Skating: men's short program—Olympic Center........ 14:00
ice dance—Olympic Center 20:00
Speed Skating: men's 1,000-meter—Olympic Oval........ 10:30
Alpine Skiing: men's giant slalom 2nd run—Whiteface Mountain 10:00
Cross-Country Skiing: men's 15-kilometer combined—Mt. Van Hoevenberg........ 11:00
Biathlon: 10-kilometer individual—Mt. Van Hoevenberg........ 08:30
Luge: men's double—Mt. Van Hoevenberg........ 12:30
Awards Ceremonies—Mirror Lake........ 19:30

WEDNESDAY, FEB. 20

Figure Skating: women's compulsory figures—Olympic Center........ 08:00
Speed Skating: women's 3,000-meter—Olympic Oval 10:30
Alpine Skiing: women's giant slalom 1st run—Whiteface Mountain 10:00
Cross-Country Skiing: men's 4 x 10-kilometer relay—Mt. Van Hoevenberg........ 09:00
Ice Hockey—Olympic Center (two rinks) 13:00-13:30
16:30-17:00
20:00-20:30
Awards Ceremonies—Mirror Lake........ 19:30

THURSDAY, FEB. 21

Figure Skating: women's short program—Olympic Center 14:00
men's free skating— Olympic Center........ 19:30
Speed Skating: men's 1,500-meter—Olympic Oval........ 10:30
Alpine Skiing: women's giant slalom 2nd run—Whiteface Mountain........ 10:00
Cross-Country Skiing: women's 4 x 5-kilometer relay—Mt. Van Hoevenberg 09:00
Awards Ceremonies—Mirror Lake and Olympic Center 19:30

FRIDAY, FEB. 22

Alpine Skiing: men's slalom—Whiteface Mountain........ 10:00
Biathlon: 4 x 7.5-kilometer relay—Mt. Van Hoevenberg 09:00
Ice Hockey—Olympic Center........ 13:30
17:00
20:30
Awards Ceremonies—Mirror Lake........ 19:30

SATURDAY, FEB. 23

Figure Skating: women's free skating—Olympic Center 19:30
Speed Skating: men's 10,000-meter—Olympic Oval........ 09:30
Alpine Skiing: women's slalom—Whiteface Mountain 10:00
Ski Jumping: 90-meter—Intervale........ 12:30
Cross-Country Skiing: men's 50-kilometer—Mt. Van Hoevenberg 08:30
Bobsled: four-man 1st and 2nd runs—Mt. Van Hoevenberg 09:30
Awards Ceremonies—Mirror Lake........ 19:30

SUNDAY, FEB. 24

Bobsled: four-man 3rd and 4th runs—Mt. Van Hoevenberg 09:30
Ice Hockey—Olympic Center........ 12:00
15:30
Awards Ceremonies—Olympic Center 18:00
Closing Ceremony—Lake Placid High School Sports Stadium........ 21:30

POTENTIAL MEDAL WINNERS IN THE 1980 WINTER OLYMPICS

EVENT		POTENTIAL MEDAL WINNERS
BIATHLON		Norway, USSR
BIATHLON RELAY		USSR, Finland
BOBSLED: 2-man and 4-man.		East Germany, Italy, Switzerland
LUGE:	Men's singles	East Germany
	Men's doubles	East Germany, West Germany, Austria
	Women's singles	East Germany, West Germany
ICE HOCKEY		USSR, Czechoslovakia, USA
NORDIC SKIING:	70-meter and 90-meter ski jumping.	Karl Schnabel, Austria; Hans Aschenbach, East Germany; Jim Denney, USA; Chris McNeill, USA
	Men's cross-country skiing: 15-kilometer, 30-kilometer, 4 x 10-kilometer relay, 50-kilometer	Norway, Finland, USSR
	15-kilometer and ski jumping	East Germany
	Women's cross-country skiing: 5-kilometer, 10-kilometer and 3 x 5-kilometer relay	USSR, Finland
ALPINE SKIING:	Men's downhill	Franz Klammer, Austria; Joseph Walcher, Austria; Ron Beiderman, USA
	Men's giant slalom and slalom	Ingemar Stenmark, Sweden; Phil Mahre, USA; Steve Mahre, USA; Klaus Heidegger, Austria, Heini Hemmi, Switzerland; Andreas Wenzel, Liechtenstein
	Women's downhill	Annemarie Moser-Proell, Austria; Susie Patterson, USA; Cindy Nelson, USA; Fabienne Serrat, France
	Women's giant slalom and slalom	Annemarie Moser-Proell, Austria; Marie Theres Nadig, Switzerland; Fabienne Serrat, France; Becky Dorsey, USA; Abbi Fisher, USA; Jamie Kurlander, USA; Kathy Kreiner, Canada

SPEED SKATING:	Men's 500-meter, 1,000-meter, 1,500-meter, 5,000-meter, and 10,000-meter	Eric Heiden, USA; Peter Mueller, USA; Dan Immerfall, USA; Frode Roenning, Norway; Sten Stenson, Norway.
	Women's 500-meter, 1,000-meter, 1,500-meter and 3,000-meter	Beth Heiden, USA; Leah Poulos-Mueller, USA; Liubov Sadchikova, USSR
FIGURE SKATING:	Men's singles	Charles Tickner, USA; Robin Cousins, Great Britain
	Women's singles	Linda Fratianne, USA; Annett Poetzsch, East Germany
	Pairs	Tai Babilonia and Randy Gardner, USA; Irina Rodnina and Alexander Zaitzev, USSR
	Dancing	Natalia Linichuk and Gennadji Karponosov, USSR

MEDAL WINNERS AT THE 1976 WINTER OLYMPICS AT INNSBRUCK, AUSTRIA

FINAL MEDAL STANDINGS

	GOLD	SILVER	BRONZE	TOTAL
USSR	13	6	8	27
East Germany	7	5	7	19
United States	*3*	*3*	*4*	*10*
West Germany	2	5	3	10
Norway	3	3	1	7
Finland	2	4	1	7
Austria	2	2	2	6
Netherlands	1	2	3	6
Switzerland	1	3	1	5
Italy	1	2	1	4
Canada	1	1	1	3
Sweden	0	0	2	2
Liechtenstein	0	0	2	2
Great Britain	1	0	0	1
Czechoslovakia	0	1	0	1
France	0	0	1	1

EVENT	GOLD	SILVER	BRONZE
Biathlon	USSR	Finland	USSR
Biathlon Relay	USSR	Finland	East Germany
Bobsled: 2-man	East Germany	West Germany	Switzerland
4-man	East Germany	Switzerland	West Germany
Luge: men's singles	East Germany	West Germany	East Germany
men's doubles	East Germany	West Germany	Austria
women's singles	East Germany	East Germany	West Germany
Ice Hockey	USSR	Czechoslovakia	East Germany
Nordic Skiing:			
Ski Jumping (70-meter)	East Germany	East Germany	Austria
Ski Jumping (90-meter)	Austria	Austria	East Germany
Cross Country Skiing:			
men's 15-kilometer	USSR	USSR	Finland
men's 30-kilometer	USSR	*United States*	USSR
men's 50-kilometers	Norway	East Germany	Sweden
men's 4 x 10-kilometer relay	Finland	Norway	USSR
Nordic combined	East Germany	West Germany	East Germany
women's 5-kilometer	Finland	USSR	USSR
women's 10-kilometer	USSR	Finland	USSR
women's 3 x 5-kilometer relay	USSR	Finland	East Germany
Alpine Skiing:			
men's downhill	Austria	Switzerland	Italy
men's giant slalom	Switzerland	Switzerland	Sweden
men's slalom	Italy	Italy	Liechtenstein
women's downhill	West Germany	Austria	*United States*
women's giant slalom	Canada	West Germany	France
women's slalom	West Germany	Italy	Liechtenstein
Speed Skating:			
men's 500-meter	USSR	USSR	*United States*
men's 1,000-meter	*United States*	Norway	USSR
men's 1,500-meter	Norway	USSR	Netherlands
men's 5,000-meter	Norway	Netherlands	Netherlands
men's 10,000-meter	Netherlands	Norway	Netherlands
women's 500-meter	*United States*	Canada	USSR
women's 1,000-meter	USSR	*United States*	*United States*
women's 1,500-meter	USSR	*United States*	USSR
women's 3,000-meter	USSR	East Germany	Norway
Figure Skating:			
men's singles	Great Britain	USSR	Canada
women's singles	*United States*	Netherlands	East Germany
pairs	USSR	East Germany	East Germany
dancing	USSR	USSR	*United States*

PHOTO CREDITS

Tony Duffy: Cover, 6, 7, 10, 14, 18, 22, 26, 31, 34, 38, 39, 42, 46, 47, 50, 54, 58, 62, 66, 70, 74; New York State Department of Commerce: 1, 3, 29; United Press International: 8, 13, 17, 21, 25, 27, 33, 37, 41, 53, 69, 76; United States Alpine Ski Team: 28, 30; Wide World Photos: 61; Wisconsin State Journal: 51.